WILD SPIRIT

It's Rae's dream to sail away across oceans on her family's boat, the *Wild Spirit* — but in 1939 the world is once again plunged into conflict, and her travel plans must be postponed. When Hitler's forces trap the Allies on the beaches of Dunkirk, Rae sails with a fleet of volunteer ships to attempt the impossible and rescue the desperate servicemen. However, her bravery places more lives than her own in jeopardy — including that of Jamie MacKenzie, the man she's known and loved for years . . .

Books by Dawn Knox
in the Linford Romance Library:

DAWN KNOX

◆

WILD SPIRIT

Complete and Unabridged

LINFORD
Leicester

First published in Great Britain in 2017

First Linford Edition
published 2020

A catalogue record for this book is available
from the British Library.

ISBN 978–1–4448–4521–1

Published by
Ulverscroft Limited
Anstey, Leicestershire

Set by Words & Graphics Ltd.
Anstey, Leicestershire
Printed and bound in Great Britain by
T. J. International Ltd., Padstow, Cornwall

This book is printed on acid-free paper

1

1933

Rae had behaved with shocking rudeness.

Poking her tongue out at the boy had been an instinctive reaction, and at nine years of age, she had to admit, she was old enough to know better.

There was no excuse for her behaviour, of course, but if the boy hadn't stared at her so intently, she'd simply have ignored him.

But he *had* stared.

Even worse, he'd smiled. Well, it was more of a smirk, really, she thought.

It wasn't surprising. She knew how ridiculous she looked. Mama had insisted she wear the hideous pink coat with its black velvet collar which had been a gift from an aunt. And the indignity didn't stop there — she'd also been made to

1

wear the matching pink Robin Hood-style hat with the black feather.

On the way down to Chichester Harbour, she'd comforted herself with the thought that Papa had said she looked beautiful, although she didn't believe for one moment that he really meant it. Her brother, Joe, wasn't interested. He simply wouldn't have noticed if she'd been wearing a potato sack. She consoled herself with the thought that on the short walk from the car park to the boatyard it was unlikely they'd bump into anyone, and most importantly, not anyone they knew.

Before she left home, her mother had demanded she wear the outfit and Rae recognised Mama was not in the mood for an argument, so it'd seemed the wisest course of action. After all, if she gave in today without a fuss, she'd take the hat and coat off when she got home and bury them in her wardrobe. Mama was so busy she would soon forget about them, and in a few months, Rae would most likely have outgrown them and the problem would have gone away.

Luckily, she was the only girl in the family so her baby brother, Jack, wouldn't have to worry about the pink outfit being handed down. Although why she was worried about Jack's feelings, she had no idea. If it hadn't been for him crying most of the night, Mama might've been in a better temper and then Rae might have dared to defy her. But seeing Papa's face and his silent plea as they put their coats on had settled it. Rae allowed herself to be buttoned into the dreadful pink coat, then she'd stood patiently while the hat was carefully positioned and pinned on her blond curls and she'd nodded obediently when Mama warned her to make sure she kept clean.

'No climbing trees or . . . or . . . whatever it is you usually do to get dirty, Hannah-Rae!' Mama had said, using her full name.

She'd bitten back the insistence that she be known as 'Rae'. Today was not the day to make an issue of it.

One-year-old Jack had just started to speak, but 'Hannah-Rae' was too complicated and he'd begun to call her 'Hammeray', which everyone found charming. Joe, however, thought his brother's pronunciation hilarious and teased Rae with the stupid name, turning something which was quite amusing into torment. Why did people feel the need to embarrass others? Rae often wondered. Why was it funny to humiliate someone?

But whereas, in the end, Mama always told Joe that he should be quiet and stop teasing Rae because he was giving her a headache, no one had stopped the boy in the boatyard from staring.

If only Rae had found it within herself to ignore him. Instead, she'd poked her tongue out, and then he'd shoved her backwards. She acknowledged he probably hadn't meant to push her right over. It was just unfortunate she stepped back and lost her balance, falling into a puddle on the

4

muddy ground. And for a second, as she lay there, everyone had stared at her. Even a man who was out walking his dog craned his neck to get a better look.

She'd never felt so humiliated in her life. The boy put his hand out to help her up and she ignored it, struggling to her feet herself; then in another rash moment that she was sure she'd regret for the rest of her life, she balled her fist and punched him on the nose.

★ ★ ★

To his credit, the boy hadn't tried to hit her back. He'd just stood there with a hurt expression on his face and blood dripping from his nose. For a second no one moved, then Joe broke the spell by bursting into laughter — and Rae had burst into tears.

'Enough!' shouted Papa. 'Rae, apologise immediately! And Joe, be quiet! I'm ashamed of you both. You obviously can't behave, so the pair of you can go and sit in the car while I see the boat. You've been so ill-mannered today, I've a good mind to cancel the order. Neither of you deserve it.'

Joe gasped at the thought of being deprived of the dinghy he'd been longing for, and looked at Rae as if it was her fault it was in jeopardy.

'Please, Papa, I'm really sorry,' Joe said.

'It's not me you ought to be apologising to!'

'I'm sorry, Mr MacKenzie,' Joe said to the owner of the boat builder's, who took the pipe from his mouth and nodded.

'Go and get in the car, Joe, and I don't want to hear another sound from you until we get home.' He turned to Rae. 'Well, missy, what have you got to say for yourself?' Despite the apparent invitation to speak, she recognised that if she dared say anything other than sorry, he would be furious.

Her humiliation was complete. There was nowhere further to sink. Mr

MacKenzie, Papa, the boy and even the man who was walking the dog were all staring at her, waiting for her to utter the words *I'm sorry.* She looked down at her coat: it was muddy and bloody. When she got home, Mama would be furious. And although Joe wouldn't dare say anything in the car, he wouldn't forget this and he'd make sure all his school friends heard about it too.

There was only one thing she could do to stop everyone looking at her. 'I'm sorry,' she whispered.

'That was a poor excuse for an apology, Rae,' Papa said sternly.

A tear slipped down her cheek. 'I'm very sorry,' she said loudly. 'I hope I didn't hurt you.'

The boy smiled at her.

'Shake the lass's hand, Jamie,' Mr MacKenzie said in his lilting Scottish accent.

The boy held out his hand.

For a second, Rae considered ignoring it, turning and walking away; but she, too, was desperate for the boat, and if there was any danger of Papa cancelling his order . . .

She shook Jamie's hand. Then without making eye contact, she turned and walked back to the car with as much dignity as she could muster.

'Are you all right, Jamie?' Papa asked the boy.

'Yes, thank you, sir.'

'Good lad!' Mr MacKenzie said. 'That lass of yours can certainly pack a punch,' Rae heard him say to Papa, although she could hear more displeasure than admiration in his voice.

★ ★ ★

'Satisfied?' asked Joe when Rae got back to the car. His arms were crossed and he glared at her.

'D'you think Papa really will cancel the boat?' she asked.

Joe shrugged. 'Well if he does, it's your fault and I'll never forgive you.'

No one spoke on the journey back to the small village of Barlstead, about five miles from MacKenzie and Sons Ltd. Boat Builders, near Dell Quay on the Fishbourne Channel. When Papa pulled into the drive of their house, Mama was waiting at the front door, holding Jack.

She shrieked when Rae got out of the car. 'What on earth happened to you? I thought I told you not to get dirty. You're filthy! Is that blood? Good grief, Hannah-Rae, are you hurt?'

Rae shook her head.

'She punched someone,' Joe said as he walked past his mother.

'You *punched* someone?'

There was no point denying it. 'Yes, Mama, I'm afraid I did.'

Rae went straight to her bedroom. She knew she'd be sent there anyway, so she decided to save her mother the trouble.

It was several weeks before either Joe or Rae were allowed to join Papa on his trips to MacKenzie's boatyard to see how their dinghy was progressing. The fact that Papa had continued to drive to the yard each weekend reassured Rae that he hadn't cancelled the order, but what would be the point of having a splendid sailboat if she wasn't allowed to use it?

But one Saturday morning, Papa had suggested a trip to Chichester Harbour to see the boat, and Rae and Joe had been overjoyed. Mama had been too busy with Jack to supervise what Rae wore. There'd been oil in the puddle she'd fallen into and the stains in the pink coat had never come out. The hat didn't go with anything else, so Rae had pushed it to the back of a drawer and hoped Mama would forget about it.

Thankfully, it was a sunny day and Rae chose a blue skirt and white blouse which she considered suitable to wear to a boatyard. She wouldn't stand out and no one would have any reason to notice her. If that dreadful boy, Jamie MacKenzie, was at the boatyard, she'd simply ignore him. She'd been practising in the mirror and she'd now perfected the expression which she'd use if he was there. It involved lifting her chin so her gaze would be aimed somewhere over his head as if she couldn't see him.

Mama stayed home with Jack, so it was just Papa, Rae and Joe who set out to check on the progress of the boat.

'D'you think it'll be ready for us to sail during the summer holidays, Papa?' Rae asked as he pulled out of the drive into the lane.

'Yes, it's almost finished now. That's why I brought you both. I'm assuming you've both learned some manners since the last time you came. Especially you, Rae.'

'Yes, Papa. I'm really sorry,' Rae said, hoping she sounded convincing.

She glanced about as they entered the yard, looking for Jamie, but thankfully he was nowhere to be seen.

Mr MacKenzie came out of his office and wiped his huge hands on his apron.

'It's good to see you again, Dr Kingsley . . . and you two,' he said, smiling at Joe and Rae and shaking Papa's hand. 'I think you're going to be pleased with the progress we've made.' He led them to the boat.

Rae was thrilled. It was nearly finished.

Papa suggested she and Joe go for a walk around the harbour and look at the other boats while he sorted out the finances for the dinghy in Mr MacKenzie's office. Rae was pleased to leave the yard, dreading Jamie appearing at any moment, and it was pleasant to walk along the waterfront admiring the boats.

'Look, there's that boy you thumped,' Joe said, pointing ahead to a lone figure who was fishing off the harbour wall.

Rae stopped and watched in amazement as Joe kept walking towards him. 'Where are you going?' she called as loudly as she dared, hoping the boy wouldn't hear her.

'Where does it look like I'm going?' Joe called over his shoulder. 'I want to see if he's caught anything.'

Rae sat on a bench and pretended to watch the yachts bobbing on the water. Without turning her head, she watched the two boys out of the corner of her eye. Jamie was showing Joe his fishing rod and allowing him to have a go. Rae wondered how long Papa would be. It seemed he'd been with Mr MacKenzie for ages. How long did it take to pay for something? she wondered.

'Rae!' Joe called. 'Come and look at this!'

She pretended she hadn't heard, and turning her head away from them, she hoped she gave the appearance of being lost in thought whilst admiring the yachts in the harbour.

Suddenly, she realised Jamie had packed up his fishing things and the two boys were walking towards her. She'd simply have to wait until they got to her. It would look too obvious if she got up and walked off. Anyway, Joe would probably only shout at her to stop. She pretended to see them for the first time and watched as they approached. Joe was a year older than Rae and she guessed that Jamie was of a similar age. They were as tall as each other, but where Joe was blond like her, Jamie was dark. He was explaining something to her brother, holding his hands apart as if demonstrating how large something was; and then as both boys began to laugh, she saw how handsome Jamie was. He had a friendly, open face with dark eyes and thick lashes. Joe stopped when they reached the bench and Rae stood up to say hello, but Jamie kept walking.

'See you, Joe,' he said, and with a slight nod in her direction to acknowledge her presence, he rearranged his fishing gear and walked towards his father's yard.

'How rude!' said Rae, watching Jamie saunter away.

'Yes, you are rude!' said Joe.

* * *

On the Saturdays when Papa wasn't on duty at the London Hospital where he worked, the Kingsley family sat down to breakfast together. Most weekday mornings he left home early to catch the train to London and often returned quite late, so Rae didn't see him much during the week. Years ago he'd met Mama when she was a nurse, but she'd stopped working when they got married, although she often talked about applying for a nurse's post when Jack started going to school. For the last few years she'd tried to keep her knowledge current, and in the evenings, Rae often found her in Papa's study going over her nursing books.

When Rae woke on Saturday, she got out of bed, washed and dressed quickly because not only was today one of Papa's Saturdays at home, but it was the day that she and Joe would be allowed to sail their new boat for the first time. A quick glance out of the window showed her the weather was favourable. The sun was still low, but there were no clouds and the wind barely moved the leaves in the trees at the bottom of the garden. There would be more of a breeze down by the coast, she was sure, and the sailing would be perfect.

And first, there would be breakfast

together. Mrs Bolton, who came in to help Mama cook and clean the house, was in the kitchen humming a tune that Rae didn't recognise. It wasn't surprising because Mrs Bolton's version of any tune varied greatly from the original, but at least she sounded happy, and she smiled at Rae when she offered to help. Mama, Papa and Jack arrived shortly after and then a tousle-haired Joe.

Everyone was in a good mood and it was hardly surprising, thought Rae. She and Joe were looking forward to sailing the new boat, and Mama and Papa were enjoying the family time and the prospect of an afternoon out together. And who knew why Jack was happy. Perhaps it was the boiled egg he'd smeared over his face. But all was right with the world . . . until Mama said she had an announcement.

She took a letter from her pocket and read the contents out loud. It seemed that she had gained a place to study medicine at the Royal Free Hospital in London.

'Isn't your mama clever?' Papa said, the pride shining in his eyes.

'So, you're going back to school?' asked Rae with a frown, unable to understand why anyone would choose to study rather than to be outside doing something interesting.

'I'm going to be a doctor,' said Mama. 'I've always longed to study medicine. My mother forbade me, so I went into nursing. She didn't really want me to do that either, but in the end I did it anyway.' She and Papa laughed.

Rae was amazed. Mama had defied her mother and now she was laughing about it! This was unbelievable!

'So,' added Papa, 'there will be a few changes. Mama will be spending a lot of time in London, and when she's at home she'll have a lot of studying to do.'

More chores! thought Rae. *She's going to say I need to do more in the house. Or perhaps she's going to ask Mrs Bolton to come in more often.*

'So we thought it would be best if we

had a live-in nanny to look after Jack,' said Papa.

'Someone living in? Oh no!' said Rae, sure it would mean more rules and restrictions.

'But it won't bother you, dear,' said Mama. 'Well, only at the weekend. You and Joe'll be boarding at your schools during the week.'

'Boarding? But I don't want to board!' Rae was horrified.

'I do!' said Joe. 'I think it's splendid!'

'It's only from Monday to Friday, Rae,' said Papa. 'You'll come home at the weekend if you want to.'

'If I want to? Of course I'd want to! I don't want to go away at all!'

'Well, it's all sorted,' said Mama, her mouth setting into a hard line. 'I thought you'd be pleased for me, Hannah-Rae.'

'My name is Rae!'

'Stop shouting!' said Mama. 'You're upsetting Jack.'

★ ★ ★

The shouting, however, had continued for some time. Mrs Bolton hastily washed up and left. 'Got enough problems of me own, I don't need to listen to all that noise!' she muttered as she tied her scarf under her chin and grabbed her basket before leaving early.

Jack had cried, not understanding the sudden change in atmosphere, and Mama had taken him to the bathroom to quieten him down and to clean the egg off his face.

Joe had gone back to his bedroom with a smile. He'd begged to be allowed to board at Bishop's Hall Boys' School for some time, since all his friends were boarders, but until now his requests had been denied.

Only Rae and Papa were still at the breakfast table.

'No, Rae, of course we don't want to get rid of you! You're being melodramatic! That's not it at all! Mama has worked so hard for this. Surely you can see that it's not going to be possible for her to do all the things she does now and study at the same time?'

Rae wasn't sure what 'melodramatic' meant, but she knew her claim that she wasn't wanted had upset Papa.

'But I'd do more in the house. And Mrs Bolton might come in for longer,' she said.

'We've already asked her and she said she can't. And after this morning, I'm not sure she'll come back at all. You know how she hates it when when things get heated.'

'You mean when Mama shouts.'

'Rae! You've done your fair share of shouting this morning too! You're more like your mother than you know!'

Rae stared at him, aghast.

Before she could contradict him, Papa reached out and holding her hand, he smiled at her. 'Perhaps this will please you. I was saving the best piece of news till last. I've named the new boat in honour of you and Mama.'

'What've you called her?' Rae asked, allowing herself to be distracted from the thought of boarding school.

'You'll have to wait and see.'

Rae was fairly certain it would be *Ray of Sunshine*, which was what Papa often called her. That would be a perfect name for a boat, but he'd said she had been named after Mama too.

'You haven't called her *Hannah-Rae*, have you?' she asked anxiously. What was the point trying to stop people calling her that if the boat was a reminder?

Papa shook his head and smiled mysteriously. 'You're just going to have to wait, I'm afraid, my little ray of sunshine.'

Ray of Sunshine! That must be it! She must have guessed the boat's name correctly.

However, later when Rae was hunting for her shoes, she overheard Papa and Mama talking in the living room.

' . . . she'll see sense eventually, Amelia, I'm sure of it. Just leave it to me,' Papa said.

Who were they talking about, and what was Papa going to do to make her

21

see sense? Of course he could have been referring to someone Rae didn't know, but the most likely explanation was either Mrs Bolton, who regularly handed in her notice, usually when Mama had upset her — which was an increasingly frequent occurrence — or indeed, Rae herself. And why was Papa so certain the unknown person would be so quick to see sense? She didn't hear any more because the sound of Joe galloping down the stairs two at a time stopped the conversation in the living room.

The picnic basket Mrs Bolton had been going to pack for them before she'd walked out was only half-prepared, and it was decided that since the quarrel at breakfast had unsettled Jack, who would now not let Mama out of his sight, they would both remain at home. Papa would take Joe and Rae and instead of a picnic, he'd buy lunch for them in the harbour café.

To prevent squabbling about who was to sit in the front when Mama wasn't in the car, Papa always insisted they sit in the back, and now, while Joe was whistling a tune, Rae stared out of the window at the blur of the hedgerows and the occasional glimpse of cows in a field. From time to time, Joe asked a question about boarding in September and Papa replied, but Rae was silent.

'Is there anything you'd like to ask, Poppet?' Papa asked her.

Before she could think, she replied 'No.' And turned her head further away from him, because she knew he would be able to see her brimming eyes in the rear-view mirror. Why had she been so stubborn? There were a lot of things she wanted to know.

Papa pulled into a lay-by and stopped the car, then turning so he could look at her, he said, 'I have a feeling there are things you'd like to ask me, Rae.'

'Why've we stopped?' asked Joe. 'There're several miles to go. Oh, we haven't broken down, have we?'

'No, son. I just need to have word with your sister and it's hard to do that without looking at her.'

Joe grunted, crossed his arms and sank back into the seat. 'Typical Rae! She always has to spoil things!'

Normally such an unfair comment would have caused an angry retort from Rae, but there was a lump in her throat and she wasn't sure the words would come out.

'You're obviously not happy, Poppet, so it's probably best we sort this out now and then you can enjoy the rest of the day.'

Rae shrugged as if she wasn't happy about discussing it but she'd do it for her father's sake.

'I need you to understand that Mama has done something remarkable.'

'Remarkable?'

'Yes, Poppet. It wasn't many years ago that women weren't allowed to study medicine, and now your mother has won a place to medical school. You should be very proud.'

'Women weren't allowed? Whyever not?'

'Because men were in charge of the

selection process and for a variety of reasons, they decided women weren't capable of becoming doctors.'

Despite herself, Rae was now interested. 'But that's awful, Papa.'

'I know. And that's why we need to do all we can to encourage Mama. When you've finished school, Mama and I will help you to do whatever you want to do. And hopefully by then, there'll be even more opportunities for girls than there are now. But until then, Mama needs your support.'

'Why can't I stay home and support her? Why do I have to board?'

'Because in order to study, Mama needs to know you're all safe. And you know how reckless you can be, Poppet. You're worse than Joe was at your age. If you two are looked after at school, then she'll be able to concentrate on her studies. Why can't you be pleased like Joe?'

'Because Joe's got lots of friends at school who're already boarders. I haven't.'

'Well, I'm sure you'll soon make

some. And you can always come home each weekend.'

'But we'll have a stranger living with us.'

'Jack needs someone to care for him. And I'm sure in time, we'll all get used to having a nanny in the house. You might even like it.'

'Can we go now?' Joe asked, scowling at his sister.

'Can we, Poppet?' Papa asked. He wasn't asking for her permission to move; she knew he was probing to find out if she was going to continue to sulk and make their lives difficult.

'I s'pose so,' she said.

Papa drove the rest of the way to MacKenzie and Sons, and while Joe resumed his shrill whistling, Rae tried to adjust to the changes ahead.

Perhaps she would like the new nanny. And if not, perhaps she could just ignore her. And if school got too bad, she'd simply run away. She'd done it before, although admittedly, she'd always returned home before nightfall.

But this time, she was older and she was sure she'd make a better job of it.

Papa took her hand when she got out of the car and she walked along beside him, enjoying the feeling of togetherness. This was the sort of thing she'd miss when she was boarding, but it wasn't like Papa was there to hold her hand during the week. He left before she was up in the morning and returned after she'd gone to bed. And at the weekend, she had to vie for his attention with Jack and Joe. So perhaps it was sensible not to fight while she had him to herself. And to think he'd named the boat after her! Well, not exactly after her, because he'd said it was for Mama too, but it made her feel special. She wondered if it involved the name 'Poppet', because he sometimes called Mama that too. Yes! That was it! It would be something like *The Sea Poppet* or *Jolly Poppet* or even *Sunshine Poppet*, which would incorporate his special name for his ray of sunshine.

27

She wanted to skip beside him to the boat which was now moored in the harbour, but she was too old for such silliness. Joe had run ahead and had obviously found the new dinghy as he waved delightedly and climbed on to it. Rae walked with Papa. She was enjoying feeling her hand in his; it made her feel safe and protected.

Finally, they were close enough to see the name of the boat. There must be some mistake, thought Rae. Joe must be on the wrong boat because this one was called *Wild Spirit*.

'I thought you said you'd named if after Mama and me,' she whispered.

'I did!' said Papa. 'I think it captures you and Mama exactly!'

Wild Spirit! Was that what he thought of her? Something savage and vicious like an animal?

Even the thought of sailing the new boat couldn't make up for the hurt she'd experienced that day.

* * *

Mama's father arrived the following afternoon.

Pop, as the children called him, dropped in periodically, but he'd come specially to congratulate his daughter on her acceptance into medical school.

Since Mrs Bolton had failed to appear that morning, Papa helped Mama clear the plates and cups from the table, accompanied by Jack, who was still unwilling to let his mother out of his sight, holding up his arms and pleading 'Carry hold, Mama, carry hold' in a wavering voice. Joe had disappeared upstairs to his room to add the stamps Pop had given him to his collection, and only Rae remained with her grandfather at the table.

'So, my darling, you must be very proud of your mama.'

'Yes,' said Rae without much conviction; then realising how half-hearted she'd sounded, she added, 'I am . . . '

'But?'

'Well, I *am* proud. It's just that I don't know why I can't stay home. I wouldn't be any trouble.'

'Trouble is your middle name, my darling! Remember last summer when you fell out of that tree? I don't know how you didn't break anything. Nor when you fell off that roof. And what about that horse? What were you thinking?'

'But Pop! I'm older now. If it meant I didn't have to board, I'd be really good.'

'Hmm. I know you mean to be good, Rae, but sometimes you act without thinking, and that's when the problems arise. Your parents have to make sure you're safe at all times — well, as safe as anyone can keep you — and that's why they need to send you to school.'

'Couldn't I come and live with you, Pop?'

He sighed sadly. 'If only that could be, my darling. I'm a bit disorganised at the moment and I'm often away on business. But you know, throughout my life, I've discovered that things are rarely as dreadful as you expect them to be. You might find you really enjoy boarding. And if not, well, you'll be home at the weekend. I know that at your age even a day seems like a long time — but trust me, my darling, the older you get, the faster time flies.'

Her shoulders slumped. Staying with Pop had been her last resort, but it looked like she had no other option but to do as everyone wanted.

'What is it you're afraid of, darling?'

'Afraid? I'm not afraid!' she said, sitting up straight and pushing out her lower jaw.

'Good gracious, you look like a bull-dog!' Pop said with a laugh. 'There's nothing wrong with being afraid, you know. Everyone's scared of something. So let me rephrase my question. What is it that you're not looking forward to?'

'I don't like any of the girls who board, so I'm going to be on my own a lot of the time. And I don't like the thought of a stranger in our house. Suppose I don't like her? Suppose she doesn't like me?'

'As you go through life, darling, there

will be plenty of people you don't like — trust me, I know. But part of growing up is learning to live with and respect people you don't actually want as your friends. It's an important lesson.'

'I s'pose . . . ' said Rae.

'I suspect, darling, that it's change that's bothering you, rather than who you might or might not be friendly with.'

'I s'pose . . . '

'There's no getting away from change. Life's all about changing and growing.'

'That's what my teacher says.'

'A wise woman!'

'She says if life doesn't change, it's called death.'

'Ah well, that's a bit more brutal than I had in mind, but I suppose there's truth in that.' Pop looked uncomfortable.

'Oh I'm sorry, Pop — did that remind you of Gran?'

'Gran?'

Rae was sorry she'd mentioned Pop's wife, her grandmother. There was always an awkward silence whenever the subject came up, and she didn't usually mention her, although she'd love to know about her. Even Mama was strangely quiet when anyone referred to her mother.

'Another cuppa, Pop?' Mama called from the kitchen.

He sighed. 'Perhaps later, thanks, love. Rae and I are just going to admire the garden.' He rose and Rae took the hand he held out to her. 'It's about time you knew about your gran. It might help you deal with your current situation, too.'

* * *

'Swing?' Pop asked.

Rae sat on the wooden swing and allowed herself to be pushed. It was something they'd done when she was younger, and although she now prided herself on being able to throw her legs out and then backwards and gain enough momentum to go quite high on her own, she knew Pop enjoyed the thought she was still a little girl.

He cleared his throat and she knew he was struggling to find words. Finally he began, 'What do you know about your gran, darling?'

'Nothing, really. I know she had two children, Mama and Uncle David. And that she died a while ago.'

'Hmm. Well, Ivy and I definitely had two wonderful children. But . . . your grandmother is still alive. It's just that Ivy and I don't live together anymore.'

'She's still alive?' Rae was shocked. 'But why don't we ever see her?'

'Because your mother fell out with her and doesn't want anything to do with her.'

Rae put her feet on the ground and stopped the swing. She looked round at Pop. 'B-But that's dreadful. How could Mama be so heartless? And what about Joe, Jack and me? We've not been allowed to meet our own gran!'

'Whoa! Hold your horses there, Rae. If you'd ever met your gran, you'd have some idea why she and your mama fell out. She's a bitter, cold-hearted woman, and it was her fault entirely that her daughter walked out.'

'She walked out on her mama?' Rae's voice rose with indignation.

'Ivy was a harsh and critical mother. Nothing David or your mother did was ever good enough. Davy ran away and joined the army as soon as he could. He's now happily married in India. Your mother desperately wanted to study medicine. Not the easiest of careers to follow for a woman, but she was extremely bright at school and I have no doubt that if Ivy and I had backed her, she'd have got into medical school and would now be as successful as your father. But Ivy didn't want her daughter to study or to work; she insisted that well-brought-up girls should marry, and she made things so difficult for your mother that one day she packed her things and left.'

'Didn't you try to stop her?'

'Unfortunately I was often away travelling on business, and to my shame, I tried to avoid all the arguments. I wish I'd put my foot down . . . but it's too late now. It's all water under the bridge.

Anyway, I have a feeling it wouldn't have made much difference to the outcome. Once Ivy made up her mind about something, there was no changing it. Davy fell in love with a lovely girl from around the corner, but according to Ivy, her family weren't good enough, and in the end she made Davy's life so miserable that he left and joined up. I haven't seen him since he went to India. He has two children who I've never met. And Ivy doesn't know about them.'

'Does she know about Joe, Jack and me?'

Pop shook his head sadly, 'No, I'm afraid not. Your mama cut all ties when she walked out. And I have to respect her decision.'

'Where's Gran now?'

'Much to her annoyance, she's still living in the East End of London, in our family home.'

'Why does that annoy her?'

'Because she thinks it's beneath her. I've always been a big disappointment to her because I never earned enough to give her all the things she wanted. Her parents were quite wealthy, and they were against her marrying me because they said I wasn't good enough for her. And they were probably right.'

'Oh, Pop!'

'Ivy thought her father would get used to the idea of us marrying, and eventually forgive her, and perhaps buy us a house somewhere. But he didn't. He cut her off without a penny, and when she realised how difficult life really was, she started to resent me. I worked had to give her all the things she wanted but I was never going to be able to provide everything she thought she deserved. I spent longer and longer working to make extra money, and after a while, I realised how much I enjoyed being away and how I dreaded going home, knowing the minute I walked through the door I'd face complaints and criticism. If it hadn't been for your mama and Davy, I think I'd simply have walked away. But looking back on it, I should have spent more time at home with my children.'

He was still behind the swing, pushing her, and although Rae couldn't see his face, she heard his voice break and knew he was deeply upset. The chains of the swing squealed rhythmically as they moved back and forth, back and forth, in the suspension rings of the frame while she waited for him to carry on.

Finally he said, 'I'm very lucky your Mama still wants me in her life.'

'Why didn't I know any of this, Pop?'

'Because it's a tale of failure and disappointment, and I'm not proud of how my life turned out. It's not something I'd normally speak about, especially not to someone so young. I'm only telling you now, darling, because I want you to understand how stubbornness and pride can tear families apart. You've inherited your strong character from your mother and your grandmother. But you have a choice. Either you use your strength to bully and hurt those who are closest to you, like your grandmother, or you put your energy into something meaningful, like your mother. Only you can decide.'

Rae was silent for a while, thinking about the bullying gran she'd never met and her mother who seemed to blow up at the slightest thing. So she'd inherited her personality from them! It'd never occurred to her before that she was like Mama. But even worse, she'd now discovered she resembled her gran, a woman who'd made not only her mother's life miserable but her gentle grandad too.

I'm not like them, she thought although deep down she wasn't sure.

'Pop?' she said finally.

'Hmm?'

'Would you say I'm wild?'

'Wild? In what sense?'

'Like a wild spirit.'

'Hmm, let me see. Well, yes, in that you're untamed, independent and free-thinking. Why?'

'Papa said he named the boat *Wild Spirit* after Mama and me. And at first, I was upset because I thought he meant we were beastly like wild animals.'

'No, darling; your papa adores you and your mama. I don't believe he meant wild as in savage. He wouldn't risk upsetting either of you. I think he was simply praising your energy and your passion, and sometimes your unpredictability.'

'What does that mean, Pop?'

'Unpredictability?'

Rae nodded.

'When you're unpredictable, it means it's impossible for anyone else to tell with any certainty what you're about to do next.'

That's me all right, thought Rae, *and sometimes I even take myself by surprise.*

'Had enough, darling?' Pop asked.

Rae nodded, and jumping off the swing, she landed lightly on the lawn.

'So, Pop, are you telling me I have to be happy about boarding and having a nanny?' she asked, taking his hand.

'Good gracious, no, darling! After what I've told you about the mess I made of my life, it would be a bit much for me to tell you how to live yours! I just wanted you to know how your Mama missed out when she was young. It's up to you to decide how to behave.'

* * *

The following day when Rae arrived home from school, Mrs Bolton opened the door.

'Yer mam's gone to London for the afternoon,' she said over her shoulder as she hurried back to the kitchen.

Rae followed, wondering why the usually slow-moving Mrs Bolton was rushing. Perhaps she had something in the oven that was burning? Rae soon realised why she wanted to get back to the kitchen.

'That's enough of the flour, young Master Kingsley! That pastry'll be as hard as a rock!' said Mrs Bolton as she took the dredger from the chubby fist. 'Now, let's get that rolling pin working, shall we?'

For all her grumbling and complaining, she obviously adored Jack, and from the mess over the table, she'd been entertaining him all afternoon.

Mrs Bolton poured Rae a glass of milk and gave her a warm jam tart.

'Young Jack didn't get his hands on that one, so don't you worry,' she said.

'What's Mama gone to London for?' Rae asked.

Mrs Bolton shrugged and sniffed, her usual way of conveying displeasure or disapproval. 'She's gone to one of them fancy agencies to find a . . . ' She paused and gave a theatrical nod towards Jack.

'Oh, you mean a nanny,' Rae said.

'Shh! Don't upset the little man!' Mrs Bolton said, looking at Jack fearfully. 'Poor little mite! Fancy getting some stranger in to look after 'im!'

'Mama!' said Jack as he heard the scrape of the key in the front door lock.

'Did you find a nanny?' Rae asked as her mother came into the kitchen.

'I've narrowed it down to two women, and they're coming here tomorrow for an interview and to meet Jack. Hopefully I'll have someone by the end of the day.' Mrs Bolton shrugged and sniffed.

★ ★ ★

When Rae returned home from school the following day, she was just in time to see a woman come out of the drive, tuck her umbrella under her arm and pull on a pair of gloves. This was obviously a woman who meant business. With a glance up at the clouds, she adjusted her hat and then marched towards Rae.

'Good afternoon,' she said in a stern voice of the sort that a teacher might use to a class of badly behaving children.

Rae greeted the miserable-looking woman politely, and turned to watch as she strode towards the bus stop, desperately hoping Mama hadn't employed her to be Jack's new nanny.

Her mother had seen her and was waiting at the door.

'Is she Jack's new nanny?' Rae asked.

'I'm not sure. She's got some excellent references. But there's still someone else to interview.'

The next candidate arrived half an hour later. Rae watched from an upstairs window as a tall, gaunt woman walked up the drive, her shapeless brown coat flapping around skinny legs. She rang the doorbell twice and Rae smiled, knowing this annoyed Mama. Not a promising start!

Rae crept onto the landing and listened to her mother greet the lady, whose name was Miss Prescott, and invite her into Papa's study. The door was ajar and Rae crept halfway down the stairs to listen to the interview. She expected Mama to ask lots of things, but it seemed that Miss Prescott was keen to get her questions in first.

'Is there a Methodist church in the vicinity, Mrs Kingsley? I couldn't consider a post which didn't have one within easy travelling distance,' she said.

'A . . . a church? Well there's St Luke's in the vill — '

'No, it must be a Methodist church. I'm afraid I don't hold with the Church of England.'

'I see. Well, now I think about it, I believe there's one in Ribbenthorpe. That's only a few miles away.'

'I can see from your reply, Mrs Kingsley, that you are not of the Methodist persuasion.'

'Err, no, I'm afraid not.'

'I see. Well, I assume you will be happy for me to carry out Bible instruction with young master Kingsley.'

'Err, well, I believe he's a little young at the moment — '

'If you don't mind me saying so, Mrs Kingsley, children are never too young to learn about the Good Book.'

'No, indeed not. Well, perhaps we could discuss your previous employers . . . '

The key turned in the lock and Joe opened the front door. 'What are you doing there?' he asked Rae loudly when he saw her on the stairs, despite her waving her hands to silence him.

Mama shut the study door and the interview carried on in private.

When Rae told Joe what she'd heard, he shrugged. 'I hope she doesn't get the job. But even if she does, I won't see her. I'm going to stay at school over the weekend. Lots of the chaps do. I'm really looking forward to it. I don't know why you're making such a fuss about boarding, Rae. If you stayed at school, you wouldn't see her or whoever gets the job. It's Jack I feel sorry for.'

Rae sighed. 'But you've got lots of friends at school. Most of my friends don't board.'

'Well, make new ones who do!' he said, and then in a rare moment of brotherly affection, he put his arm around her shoulder. 'Look, Rae, we break up on Thursday and we've got weeks to do exactly what we like. Don't spoil it by worrying about next term.'

She smiled. 'Yes, I suppose you're right.'

'Atta girl! We've got lots of serious

sailing to do in *Wild Spirit* before we go back for the autumn term. And I'm going to prove to the world I'm a much better sailor than you!'

Rae punched him playfully on the arm. 'You don't stand a chance, brother dear!'

After Miss Prescott had left, Rae asked her mother whether she'd chosen a nanny.

'Well, I want to discuss it with Papa first,' she said, 'but I think I prefer the first one I interviewed.'

Rae wasn't sure whether to be relieved or not. The woman she'd passed in the lane outside their house had looked and sounded rather severe, and it was possible she wasn't any nicer than Miss Prescott. But it seemed it was up to Papa now.

The next morning, Rae got up early hoping to catch Papa before he left for work, but he'd already gone.

'What did Papa say about the nanny, Mama?'

'Hmm? Oh, he said it was up to me.'

'And what've you decided?'

'The first one, Mademoiselle Thérèse Jacquet. I'll see if she can come back today so you and Joe can meet her.'

Mademoiselle Thérèse Jacquet. Such a pretty name for such a miserable-looking woman.

Rae described the new nanny to Joe as they walked together to the bus stop.

'She's probably much nicer when you get to know her,' said Joe. 'And I suppose we'll find out later.'

After school that afternoon, they got off the bus together at the stop near their house.

'Race you home!' said Joe, setting off before he'd spoken so he got ahead start, but for once Rae didn't take up the challenge. She was in no rush to see the new nanny. When she let herself in the front door, Joe was just coming out of the living room, his eyes wide in astonishment, and he closed the doors carefully behind him.

'Wait till I tell the chaps at school about this!' he whispered as he tousled her hair.

'Stop it!' she squealed, which made him rub her head harder.

'Rae? Is that you?' Mama called from the living room. 'Come and say hello to Mademoiselle Jacquet.'

As Rae opened the door, she caught sight of herself in the mirror above the fireplace and was horrified at her reflection, which showed that her blond curls were in even more of a mess than usual.

'Rae! What have you been up to?' Mama asked crossly. 'Really, you could have tidied yourself up before you came to meet Mademoiselle Jacquet.'

Rae looked around for the barrel-shaped lady with the severe face she'd seen yesterday, but the only other person in the room was an elegantly dressed young woman in her early twenties who was holding out a beautifully manicured hand. 'Good afternoon, I am very pleased to meet you,' she said in a soft French accent.

* * *

49

'Honestly, Rae, you might have been a bit more welcoming to the new nanny! I know you're not happy about us having one, but that's no reason to be rude. Fancy staring at her like that! I was so embarrassed!'

'I'm sorry, Mama, but I thought you said you'd decided to accept the first woman who came for interview. When I got home from school yesterday, I saw a large woman come out of our house and I thought it was her. She looked rather scary.'

'Ah, I see. That must have been Mrs Oliver. Oh, yes, I did say I was going to interview two ladies, didn't I? But the agency called early and said they had another excellent candidate and would I like to see her? Mademoiselle Jacquet came about midday. I wasn't really keen on the other two ladies, although they were extremely well qualified. But Jack seemed to take to Mademoiselle Jacquet immediately. I just hope Papa's happy. He only saw the details about the other two ladies.'

'I'm sure he'd prefer her to Mrs Oliver and Miss Prescott,' said Rae, 'and I know Joe does. He can't wait for Mademoiselle Jacquet to move in.'

* * *

Finally it was Thursday and the first day of the summer holidays. As soon as Rae awoke, she got out of bed, and after briefly wondering if Mama would notice if she didn't wash, she decided not to risk it. It would be dreadful to be sent back upstairs and to waste good sailing time. How marvellous to be able to exchange her gymslip and blazer for knee-length shorts and jumper on top of her bathing suit!

Usually slow to waken, Joe was also up early, keen to make the most of the first day of freedom. After a rushed breakfast, they put a few apples and some of Mrs Bolton's sausage rolls in Rae's bicycle basket and set off down the drive.

The sun was still low and the breeze

cool, but Rae soon warmed up as they cycled through the lanes towards Chichester Harbour.

This was going to be a perfect day.

Joe dismounted when they arrived at the waterfront and pedalled his bicycle towards MacKenzie and Sons' boatyard.

'What're you doing?' Rae called.

'Papa's arranged for us to leave our bicycles in the boatyard to keep them safe,' he called over his shoulder, 'You can do what you like with your bicycle. But if it goes missing while we're sailing, you're on your own. Don't think I'm going to give you a lift on my crossbar. You can walk!'

As Rae reluctantly wheeled her bicycle towards the boatyard, Jamie MacKenzie came out of the gate with his fishing gear. She stopped, and pretending she had a stone in her plimsol, she took it off and shook it. That boy was the last person she wanted to see. Joe hadn't let her forget the day they'd first encountered each other and the memory still made her burn with shame. If she delayed, it would give him time to go off with his fishing rod, and then she and Joe could go sailing as planned. But Joe obviously had other ideas.

'Rae!' he called. 'I've asked Jamie to come with us. Hurry up.'

She'd recently learned what she understood was a very rude word and she said it under her breath. But there was nothing for it. Now Joe had asked the boy to go with them, she'd have to put up with it, or not go sailing at all.

'Come on, Rae!' Joe yelled as he and Jamie reached the *Wild Spirit*. 'Anyone'd think you didn't want to go sailing!'

'I don't with him!' she muttered under her breath, but she hurried up anyway. Papa had forbidden either of them to sail alone, but Joe could conceivably cast off with Jamie and leave her behind.

Jamie climbed aboard first and helped Joe, then held out his hand for Rae; but ignoring it, she scrambled onto the boat herself.

'You take the tiller, Jamie,' Joe said. 'I bet you know some interesting places to go around here.'

Jamie looked at Rae to judge her reaction at him being handed the tiller, but she pretended not to care and busied herself with the jib sail while the boys chatted as they rigged the boat, completely ignoring her.

Joe untied the painter and they moved from their mooring into the open water. Jamie pointed in the direction of the creek the boys had decided they would head towards. The sails flapped then filled with wind, and Jamie turned the tiller, heading away from the harbour. Zigzagging in a series of tacks, they made good progress; and despite feeling left out, Rae thrilled as the salt-kissed breeze whipped past, blowing her hair about her face in damp tendrils.

Finally, they turned into Jamie's inlet and the wind dropped, letting the sails slacken and flap.

'Shall we make for that beach?' Jamie asked.

'Do as you like!' said Rae, upset she hadn't been consulted about anything.

She crossed her arms and looked in the opposite direction.

'For goodness sake, Rae, stop sulking!' Joe said. 'You're getting on my nerves.'

The boat rocked as he lunged, seizing her arm and throwing her off balance. For a second, it looked as though they would both topple overboard, but Joe managed to grab one of the stays. Rae, however, somersaulted into the water with a splash. She surfaced spluttering with indignation.

'What did you do that for?' she demanded. 'I'm going to tell Papa on you!'

'Oh, shut up, Rae! When I tell Papa what a spoiled brat you've been, he'll say 1 should have done it before!'

Jamie reached over the gunwale and offered her his hand to pull her out. For a second, she was tempted to refuse, but Joe was glaring at her and she wondered if he might make her swim to the beach. If she'd only been wearing a bathing suit, she wouldn't have minded, but her blouse and shorts were flapping round her arms and legs, hampering her movements.

She took Jamie's hand, but before she could think her actions through, she placed her feet against the hull; and as he leaned out to get a firmer grip, she pushed against the wooden planking as hard as she could, resulting in Jamie flying through the air into the water. Had she considered what would happen, she might've resisted the urge, because he crashed on top of her and their heads clashed together, his cheekbone against the top of her head. The force of him landing on her drove her under the water again, and the shock of the impact resulted in her gulping in a mouthful, which made her choke.

Finally, when she'd stopped coughing, she reached up to grab the gunwale of the boat and looked up at Joe, who she expected to be furious. However, he had a strange expression on his face which she couldn't read, and he appeared to be scanning the water behind her. She looked round, expecting Jamie to be bobbing on the surface but he was nowhere to be seen. Turning back to Joe, she looked at him quizzically, and he shrugged as if he was as puzzled as her and didn't know where Jamie was. The blood suddenly drained from her face as she wondered if he was still under the water.

'Joe! Oh Joe! Where is he? Has he drowned?' she wailed. But instead of diving in to help her as she swam about waving her arms underwater to search for Jamie, he turned away. Seconds later, Jamie was on deck and the two boys were almost hysterical with laughter.

★   ★   ★

Rae later learned that while she was choking, Jamie had surfaced, and after taking a deep breath, he'd dived down and swum away from her to the other

57

side of the boat. Jamie hauled himself out of the water, and when Joe saw him and realised he was paying Rae back for her bad behaviour by allowing her to believe he'd gone missing, he'd played along.

Rae was glad to get back to harbour after the dreadful outing. It had looked so promising that morning when they'd set off from home. It was always that horrible boy who spoiled things. And now he and Joe were becoming great friends. She could see that the sailing trips she'd been longing for would now always be shared with Jamie MacKenzie, and she made up her mind she'd simply stay at home.

There was something else bothering her too. She and Joe would have to go into the boatyard to retrieve their bicycles before they rode home, and she was dreading seeing Mr MacKenzie. It wouldn't take him long to see Jamie's black eye and to find out that he'd got it when she'd pulled him into the water and they'd clashed heads. But perhaps they'd be able to take their bicycles before Mr MacKenzie noticed them.

However, as soon as they entered the yard, he came out of the office to greet them. 'Ouch, laddie,' he said to Jamie, tilting his chin up so he could get a better look at the swollen black eye, 'that's a nasty shiner you've got there.'

'I slipped, Dad,' said Jamie. 'I went down like a sack of potatoes.'

Mr MacKenzie grunted and looked over his son's shoulder towards Rae. 'Well, I expect you'll be more careful next time, eh, lad?'

Rae picked up her bicycle and began to wheel it towards the gate.

'See you tomorrow, Jamie?' called Joe.

'No, sorry, Joe. Dad and I are off to Scotland early tomorrow. See you in August.'

It seemed to Rae that finally something was going her way.

★ ★ ★

'Jamie's back tomorrow,' said Joe one evening at the end of August.

'How d'you know?' Rae asked, her heart sinking at the thought of sharing Joe and the *Wild Spirit* with Jamie MacKenzie.

'It says so in his postcard, you dolt! Don't you remember? It only came last week.'

'Oh, yes,' said Rae. She'd avoided the postcard from Scotland, which still stood on the mantelpiece in the living room showing a handsome stag with heather-clad hills in the background.

The sunny days spent sailing with Joe during the week and with Papa, when he was free at the weekend, had seemed to last for months. But now, even though there were still a few days left of the summer holidays, it felt as though they were over. Rae was tempted to stay home and let Joe and Jamie sail on their own, but Mama was in an irritable mood because of the preparations for the arrival of Mademoiselle Jacquet; and Rae knew that inevitably, despite her best intentions, she'd get in the way and Mama would shout at her.

Just after the nanny arrived, Rae would be on her way back to school. The summer holidays would definitely be over.

Indeed, it felt like her life was over.

The next morning, she still hadn't made up her mind whether she'd accompany Joe sailing that day, and she decided to wait until she was ready and see how she felt. But when she went into the kitchen for breakfast, Mrs Bolton, who was frying bacon, looked up warily.

'Oh, it's you, lovey,' she said with relief. 'I thought it were your mam. What with Joe throwing up all night and young Jack playing up, she's a bit steamed up this morning. If I were you, I'd keep out o' her way.'

A white-faced Joe was lying in bed looking sorry for himself. 'Are you going to the harbour today?' he asked her.

'I don't suppose so. I can't sail on my

own. You know Papa's forbidden it.'

'Jamie'd go with you.'

'I don't like Jamie. Why would I want to spend the day with him?'

'Oh Rae, don't be such a clot! There's nothing wrong with Jamie. He's a lot of fun. And he'll be waiting for us. I've asked Mama to phone and tell his father I'm not well, and she said she'd do it later when she had time, but who knows when that'll be? And Jamie'll be waiting until then. You don't think you could telephone his father, do you?'

Mr MacKenzie was someone who Rae definitely didn't want to talk to. She knew he didn't believe his son's story about how he'd acquired the black eye, and she also knew that he suspected her of causing it.

'Oh, all right,' she said. 'I'll ride down to the harbour and tell him. I'll check the *Wild Spirit* as well, but I'm not going out sailing with him.'

'Tell him I'll get down there as soon as I'm better,' Joe said. He groaned. 'It's best you go now,' he added urgently, reaching for the bowl beside his bed.

She rushed out of his room.

Rae was relieved to see that Jamie was waiting outside his father's yard as soon as she rounded the bend. She hadn't been looking forward to bumping into Mr MacKenzie and having to endure his probing looks. But now she'd be able to deliver Joe's message and be on her way. Where she was going after she'd looked over the *Wild Spirit*, she had no idea. Perhaps she'd go to the beach, although it wasn't a place she'd ever been to on her own before.

A wave of loneliness washed over her. She didn't want to stay home because she'd undoubtedly get into a row with Mama, and she'd probably be dragged into the preparations for the new nanny, whose arrival she was dreading. With Joe sick, she couldn't go sailing, and in a few days she'd be staying at the school she loathed. She didn't seem to belong anywhere.

'You're looking a bit cross,' Jamie

said as she stopped her bicycle. 'Has Joe upset you?' He looked over her shoulder at the road. 'Where is he?'

Rae explained and relayed her brother's message about coming when he was better.

'Oh, that's a shame,' Jamie said, and she realised his Scottish accent, which had been barely noticeable before, was now stronger. 'So where are you off to now?'

'The beach,' she said decisively.

'On your own?'

'Yes!' she said, defying him to comment on her lack of company.

'D'you mind if I come?'

She hadn't expected that, and for a second she didn't know what to say.

'Only I've got something for you! I brought it home from Scotland.' He patted his pocket. 'Don't move — I'll be back in a wink,' he said, and rushed off to get his bicycle before she could tell him she didn't want him to go with her.

Rae was tempted to cycle off and

leave him behind, but the thought of having someone — anyone — to spend the day with was appealing, even Jamie MacKenzie. And he seemed different, more grown up, than he had the last time she'd seen him. There was also the question of the thing he had in his pocket for her. It was probably a half-chewed toffee or something ghastly like that, but she was now curious about what it could be.

Jamie came cycling out of the boatyard, followed by Mr MacKenzie, who told his son to be careful, then took his cap off and scratched his head as he watched them both ride off.

'Have you ever been to Cranston's Point?' Jamie called over his shoulder to Rae.

'No,' she yelled back.

'Okay, follow me!'

★ ★ ★

They propped their bicycles against the ancient stones of the ruins of the round

65

watchtower which had once looked out over the water, preventing marauders from attacking further up the river.

'It's very small,' she said doubtfully, looking at the sandy strip at the edge of the water. Indeed, it was hardly a beach at all.

He followed her gaze and seemed to see it through different eyes. 'I haven't been for a while. Alex and I always used to come here when we were younger,' he said, almost apologetically.

'Who's Alex?'

'My elder brother. Haven't you seen him at Dad's yard?'

She blushed then, when she thought of the two occasions she'd been in the yard — the first time, when she'd punched Jamie, and the second, when she'd caused his black eye. She certainly hadn't taken any notice of the men who worked there.

Jamie didn't seem to notice and carried on, 'Alex and I are the sons in MacKenzie and Sons. When I leave school, I'll work alongside Alex and Dad.'

'Is that what you want?'

'Yes . . . ' He sounded a bit doubtful. 'It's good to know I've got a place in a business once I've left school.' He paused.

'But?'

'Well, I like helping Dad in the yard, but what I'd really love to do is to sail to other countries. Perhaps even go around the world.'

'Around the world! Oh, how wonderful that would be!'

She was amazed it'd never occurred to her to do anything so adventurous, and she was envious that he'd had the idea and not her.

They sat on a large smooth rock, waiting for the sun to come round and warm the tiny ribbon of sand. Rae wondered if she wouldn't have been better off going to a beach on her own, even if it meant not talking to anyone all day. After all, what was there to say to a boy she barely knew? And one that she didn't even like. But to her surprise, they chatted easily, much like Jamie and

67

Joe had done when they'd cut her out of the conversation. Or, she mused, perhaps it wasn't that they'd cut her out of the conversation. Perhaps they'd simply been enjoying each other's company and hadn't noticed she'd been sulking.

'I'm trying to learn French out of a book,' he said, 'so that when I travel, I can talk to people — well, anyone who speaks French, anyway. But it's very hard.'

'Don't you learn French at school?'

He shook his head. 'I don't go to a private school like you and Joe. We just do the ordinary subjects at my school.'

'Oh.' It hadn't occurred to her before that learning a foreign language was something special. Something that people might *want* to do. 'We've got a French woman coming to live with us this weekend,' she said, and told him about the new nanny. And then to her surprise, she found herself suggesting he come over to their house to talk to her.

'That'd be nice,' he said. 'It'd be good to hear how French is spoken.'

'Oh, you just need to speak like *thees*,' she said with an exaggerated French accent, making him laugh. 'You know, you sound different,' she said, 'since I last saw you.'

'Yes, every time I go back to Scotland, my accent gets stronger. But it'll be back to normal soon.'

Before she could stop herself, she said, 'That's a shame. I like it.'

He looked at her then as if trying to decide whether she was laughing at him, but her blushes must have told him otherwise, and in response he reddened too.

'Oh,' he said to cover the awkwardness, 'I nearly forgot. I brought this back from Scotland for you.' He put his hand in his pocket and pulled out a small packet. 'It's not much, but it made me think of you.'

As she untied the string and opened the brown parcel paper, she hoped it wasn't a joke. *Please don't let it be something really unpleasant*, she thought.

But why would he have bought her

anything nice? The last time she'd seen him, she'd given him a black eye. It would probably be something like a spider wrapped in the white cotton material she could see inside the packet. Or something stupid like a stone.

She held it out so that whatever dreadful thing was inside wouldn't fall in her lap, and she flapped the material open.

It was a handkerchief. In the corner was a small embroidered thistle with two spiky leaves entwined to form a curlicue underneath. She stared at it.

'You don't like it,' he said with disappointment.

'Oh, I do! I do!' she said. 'I was just surprised, that's all.'

He smiled with pleasure, 'I chose it myself. It reminded me of you.'

'Me?' She was astounded to learn he'd thought of her at all while he was away — unless of course, it was with resentment.

'Yes, it was the thistle in the corner,' he said, 'it's just like you. All soft and

70

fluffy but underneath as prickly as . . . well, a thistle!'

He leaped up laughing, pretending to duck imaginary blows from her and despite her disappointment that he'd called her prickly, she couldn't help laughing too. It seemed to be an appropriate description and since he'd twice been on the receiving end of her temper, she thought, well, he was entitled to have an opinion.

When Rae went to bed that night, she lay awake for some time, going over the surprising day. What had started as a disaster, had actually been very pleasant and although she didn't wish Joe ill, she realised with a stab of guilt she didn't want him to go sailing tomorrow. She wanted to go back to the tiny beach at Cranston's Point, next to the ruined watchtower with Jamie and talk about travelling around the world. She wanted to swim with him and lay on the sand drying herself with him. And she wanted to watch his long lashes on his cheeks as he feigned sleep and she wanted to run away from him as he leaped up and chased her into the water where he swam after her, splashing wildly pretending he couldn't catch her. She hadn't laughed so much for . . . well, forever.

In her bedside drawer, she had the snail shell he'd given her. At first, she'd wanted to drop it and stamp on it in disgust but he'd said that it was a good omen to find such a shell.

'Snails carry everything they need on their backs and then they just travel about. That'll be us one day,' he'd said.

Us, she thought, Jamie had said 'Us.'

* * *

By the next morning, Joe had recovered from his stomach bug and was already on his bicycle, keen to escape the confines of the house, before Rae had even grabbed a slice of toast.

Jamie was waiting outside the yard and seemed pleased to see Joe after so long and once again, Rae felt as if she was being disregarded. They sailed in the *Wild Spirit*, and the day had passed uneventfully, much to her disappointment. The togetherness of the previous day had gone and she began to wonder if she'd imagined it. As the boys were saying their final goodbyes until the next school holidays, Joe suddenly remembered he'd left his pullover on the *Wild Spirit*, and cycled back to the boat to fetch it.

Jamie took Rae's hand, 'Will you write to me?' he asked, 'Please!'

'Yes,' she said.

Seconds later, Joe screeched to a halt next to them. Jamie had already let go of her hand and moved away.

As they cycled away from the harbour, she looked over her shoulder at the receding figure of Jamie, the boy she'd started by loathing.

And now? She wasn't sure.

What did it matter anyway? She wouldn't see him for ages. Although Mama had suggested she board during the week and return at weekends, Rae had decided to remain at school until the Christmas holidays. Home wouldn't feel like home with a nanny there and with Mama in London attending lectures or in the study, needing silence while she pored over her books.

One day, she told herself, *I'll find a place where I belong and where I feel I'm wanted.*

★ ★ ★

'Well, don't just stand there staring, Joe — go and help your father carry the luggage,' Mama said when Mademoiselle Jacquet arrived. Papa had picked her up from the railway station and was now struggling with her trunk and cases.

Mademoiselle Jacquet carried nothing more than a tiny handbag as she glided gracefully towards the front door where Mama, Rae, Jack and Joe were waiting.

'Welcome, Mademoiselle Jacquet,' said Mama, stepping forward.

'I would be very pleased if you would call me Thérèse,' the French girl said, and Mama agreed that perhaps it would be easier for Jack to pronounce.

It was as if the new nanny was an important guest and not an employee, Rae thought. Papa and Joe were fussing over the cases which she'd left to them, like one would use railway porters. Even Mama had readily agreed to the informality of calling her by her first name. Rae had no idea what Mrs Bolton's first name was, and she'd been working for the family since before Joe was born. In fact, it had never occurred to Rae that Mrs Bolton might *have* a first name.

But perhaps in France things were done differently. People certainly dressed with more style, if Thérèse was anything to go by, Rae thought. She wore a cream cape with dark blue piping which matched her dress, high-heeled shoes and gloves. Her fashionably short hairstyle was half-hidden by a cream and blue beret set at a jaunty angle, below which was a kiss-curl.

Although each garment was deceptively simple, when they were combined, Thérèse would undoubtedly turn heads. But although the clothes made her look smart, the young French woman had something extra. Exactly what it was, Rae had no idea. Perhaps it was the way she carried herself? But there was nothing rigid or stiff about Thérèse — she didn't look like a soldier on parade, which was how Rae felt when she did as Mama told her and stopped slouching. Whatever Thérèse was doing appeared to be unconscious and effortless, and the only person apart from Rae who wasn't pleased at her arrival was Mrs Bolton.

'So, my cooking isn't good enough for Miss La-de-Da!' she said to Rae, who'd helped her carry the plates into the kitchen after dinner that evening. She stood with hands on hips, glaring at the food which Thérèse had left. 'If she thinks I'm going to start cooking all that foreign muck, she's got another think coming!'

There was only one good thing about

Thérèse's arrival, thought Rae the following morning — it made leaving home much easier. There were going to be a lot of adjustments, and Rae could see there were going to be a lot of arguments too.

'That bacon's not burnt, it's just crispy!' Mrs Bolton shouted when Mama took Thérèse's breakfast plate back into the kitchen with the nanny's comment and a request for something else.

'Please be reasonable, Mrs Bolton. Thérèse is used to different food; she's just settling in. Hopefully it won't take too long.'

At least Rae would be spared any more of the 'settling in'.

Papa had taken the day off so that he and Mama could drive Joe and Rae to their respective schools, and breakfast was to be the last meal the family would share together until the school holidays. Rae looked around the table. Papa was distracted; he was probably thinking about the patients he ought to have been treating that day. Mama and Joe watched Thérèse. Rae guessed her mother was hoping she would be able to get back to her books later, and suspected Joe was not thinking about his books at all. Jack was pushing away the toast his new nanny was feeding him: 'No crusts!' he said crossly. And Thérèse glanced around the table from time to time as if weighing up the family with whom she was now living and comparing them to the people she'd left behind in Paris. Rae suspected the Kingsleys were not being compared favourably.

With her departure to school imminent, she felt like a small boat which had slipped its moorings and was slowly drifting out of the harbour with the tide, away from everything she'd ever known.

★ ★ ★

After Mama and Papa had left the school, Miss Frost, the headmistress, led Rae into her office.

'I have a special favour to ask you, Hannah-Rae,' she said. 'We have a new girl starting at St Helena's this term and as she'll be boarding, the same as you. I wondered if you'd keep an eye on her. She's been travelling the world with her parents and has just returned from Hong Kong, so she's going to need a friend to help her adjust to life at school. The two of you have been allocated one of the senior rooms rather than sleeping in the junior dormitory, so she can have a chance to get used to things. Now, how do you feel about that?'

How did she feel about that? Happier than Miss Frost could imagine! She'd been dreading the thought of sleeping in a room with so many other girls who'd never been friendly to her, but now she'd share a room with one other person.

'Fine, thank you, Miss Frost.'

'Good. Well, I'm sure I don't need to remind you, Hannah-Rae, that having one of the senior girls' rooms is a privilege, and at the first sign of either you or the new girl abusing my trust, you will be found beds in the usual dormitory. Do I make myself clear?'

'Yes, Miss Frost.'

'The girl's name is Roberta Taylor-Gale.'

'Yes, Miss Frost.'

The only possible problem would be if she and the new girl didn't get on. And that would be disastrous.

However, Roberta — or Bobby, as she insisted on being called — was the ideal roommate. She had perfected the art of having fun without drawing attention to herself and seemed to be able to charm her way out of any situation, carrying Rae with her. Although Bobby was in Rae's form, she was a year older, having missed so much schooling while she'd been travelling the world that she'd been kept back a year; but to Rae's surprise, she wasn't bothered at all.

'When I've had enough of school, I'll simply leave,' she said confidently. Rae wasn't convinced, although as the term progressed and she saw how easily Bobby got her way, she wondered if she was right.

'I'm worldly wise,' Bobby told her. 'It's all the travelling I've done.'

Rae had no idea what *worldly wise* meant, but after hearing Bobby's stories, she was more determined than ever to travel away from England, and as soon as she could.

She'd written to Jamie to tell him about Bobby and some of the exotic places she'd lived, and how wonderful it would be to visit Hong Kong with him. After checking the post each morning for a month, Rae gave up looking for a reply from Jamie. During the first fortnight, she'd written four long, newsy letters to him.

If he couldn't be bothered to reply, she wouldn't write again, she decided crossly.

★　★　★

81

The final fortnight of the autumn term passed in an excited frenzy, with teachers attempting to control the girls' high spirits as Christmas approached. Rae threw herself into the festivities and deliberately avoided thinking about going home. Joe was going to stay with his friend Geoffrey for a few days, so when she got home, things would be a bit flat. In one of Mama's infrequent letters, she'd said she was about to sit an exam, and Rae expected Papa would be busy at the hospital too. People didn't stop being sick just because it was Christmas.

Bobby had invited Rae to stay at her parents' house in London for a few days, but the week before the end of term, Bobby's father had been called to South Africa and her mother and Bobby were going to stay with relatives in Cornwall.

'You'll be back at school in January, though, won't you?' Rae asked anxiously.

'I'll be here if I have to walk all the way from Truro!'

Bobby had become so popular since she'd started at St Helena's, with her bubbly personality, that she'd soon earned the nickname Bubbles, and it seemed that simply by association, Rae had become popular too. So despite finishing the autumn term without Bobby, Rae was kept fully occupied and distracted, and successfully blocked all thoughts of home.

Pop came to pick her up on the last day of term and took her into Chichester for lunch. She was pleased to see him, of course, but also sad that neither of her parents had come.

Pop could see her disappointment and quickly made excuses — 'There's been an outbreak of flu and your father's really busy at the hospital and your mama's got a sore throat or she'd have come to pick you up. We're hoping she's not going down with the flu as well. But at least she sat her exam a few days ago and she thought it went fairly well.'

'How's Jack?' Rae asked.

'The last time I saw him, he was elbow-deep in flour in the kitchen, making pastry for mince pies.'

'Mrs Bolton's allowed Thérèse into her kitchen?' Rae asked in amazement. So the elegant French girl had even wormed her way into Mrs Bolton's good books, she thought with disappointment.

'No, darling, Thérèse isn't there. She's gone home to Paris for Christmas. Mrs Bolton's looking after Jack while your mama's not well. You know how she dotes on him.'

Suddenly, Rae longed to go home. Christmas didn't look so gloomy after all.

★　★　★

Mrs Bolton greeted Rae the following morning.

'Yer mam's not feeling too good, and she wants you and the little man out of the house so neither of you catch it. She said it's okay if you go down to the harbour if you want, so long as you don't get into mischief; or you can come with us to feed the ducks.' She

84

patted Jack on the head.

Rae decided against a trip to the village pond to watch Mrs Bolton and Jack throw bread at the ducks. She dressed warmly and cycled carefully through the lanes, avoiding any of the ice which had appeared overnight, and wondered if Jamie would be waiting outside the boatyard.

Of course he won't, she told herself, and she wondered whether she dared to peer in through the gates to see if she could catch his eye. But she knew the only person's eye she was likely to catch was Mr MacKenzie's. However, it would've been good to tell Jamie off for wasting her time, asking her to write and then completely ignoring her.

She stopped outside the harbour café and looking at her reflection in the window, she took her hat off and then pulled her hair into some sort of order with her fingertips. Then she cycled slowly around the corner. If Jamie was there, she decided she'd pass him as if she'd forgotten him, and if he spoke, she'd pretend to wonder who he was, and then perhaps she'd remember. Rae wished she'd rehearsed the whole sequence at home in the mirror because she wasn't confident she'd look believable. Perhaps she'd simply cycle past him and not stop.

Or perhaps he'd have gone to Scotland for Christmas . . .

To her amazement, Jamie was leaning against the wall of the boatyard with one leg bent and his foot pressed against the bricks. When he saw her, he stood up straight and ran towards her, a joyful smile on his face.

'I wasn't sure you were coming,' he said, and then with a look past her, he added, 'Is Joe coming?'

'No, he's gone to stay with a friend,' she said, and realised too late she hadn't put any of her plans to ignore him into action. But he'd looked so pleased to see her that it had taken her completely by surprise.

'I've been keeping an eye on the *Wild Spirit*,' he said with enthusiasm. 'D'you want to go and see her?'

'No, said Rae, cross that he seemed to think they could start where they'd left off in August. 'Not with you, anyway. I'll go on my own!'

His smile had gone and he looked so hurt that she began to regret her words.

Out of the corner of her eye, Rae saw Mr MacKenzie at the gate. He took the pipe out of his mouth and said, 'Mornin', lass. I thought I heard voices. I wondered if it were you.'

Her cheeks reddened. 'Good morning, Mr MacKenzie,' she said. 'Well, I'd better be off.'

By the time she reached the *Wild Spirit*, Jamie had got his bicycle and had caught up with her. 'I don't understand,' he said. 'Why're you so cross?'

'Because you asked me to write to you. And I did. Four long letters, and you didn't reply!'

'Ah!'

'Is that all you've got to say?' Her voice had started to rise again.

'Come with me to Cranston's Point

and I'll explain,' he said without meeting her eye.

* * *

The rock was still in shade when they arrived at the beach and propped their bicycles against the ruins.

'So?' Rae demanded.

'Well, I did try to write you a letter,' he began. 'I started lots. In the end, Dad told me off for wasting good writing paper. But . . . well, I just couldn't think of anything to say. You told me about all sorts of things at your school, but there was nothing to tell you. I went to school, I helped Alex and Dad, and then I did it all over again the next day. My school's not fancy like yours.'

'Oh,' she said. He looked so sorry that it was hard to be angry. 'But I didn't even know you'd got the letters. You could've just written and told me not much was going on.'

'Well, there's another reason.' He leaned over and picked up a pebble, which he sent hurtling into the water.

'Yes?' she prompted.

'Well, it's just that I'm left-handed.'

'So?'

'Well, my writing's awful and I smudge a lot of it. I didn't want your friends at school to laugh. I couldn't even address the envelope properly. I asked Alex to do it but he told me to get lost.'

'Oh. I wish I'd known,' she said finally. 'Only, it felt like you'd forgotten . . . ' She wanted to say 'me' but it sounded too . . . too what? She didn't know but, in the end, she finished ' . . . like you'd forgotten you asked me to write. Like you didn't care.'

He fished in his pocket and withdrew four dog-eared folded sheets of paper and opened one out. They were the letters she'd sent him.

'I did care,' he said.

'You've still got them?' she asked, incredulous that he had them in his pocket.

'Of course.'

'But why?'

He picked up another stone, and

89

jumping off the rock, he crouched low to skim it across the water. 'I just have,' he said. Then, changing the subject, he added, 'Tell me about Hong Kong. Your friend Bobby sounds so lucky.'

Before long, they were chatting as easily as they had in August. Jamie's accent had almost disappeared as he'd said it would, and when she remarked on it, he assumed a very strong Scottish accent and made her laugh. They'd planned to go to all the places Bobby had told Rae about and some more that Jamie had seen in his atlas.

As the sun began to dip towards the west, Jamie reluctantly said they'd have to go. 'It'll be dark soon.'

Rae nodded, disappointed at the shortness of the day.

'Will you come tomorrow?' he asked. His words were casual but his eyes pleading.

'I'll try.'

'Will Joe come?'

'I don't think so. Mrs Bolton said he'll be coming home about lunch time.'

Jamie smiled.

The next day when Rae arrived at the boatyard, Jamie was waiting outside, already mounted on his bicycle, and he rode off, leading the way to their beach.

'I can't stay long,' Rae said when they dismounted at the ruined tower. 'Joe'll be home this afternoon.'

'Me neither,' said Jamie. 'Dad wants me to help him with something after lunch. But we've got a few hours.'

Rae looked up at the heavy grey clouds which promised snow. 'I'm not even sure we've got a few hours.'

'Well, I'd better give you this now, then,' he said, taking a box out of the bag he'd slung over his handlebars. 'Dad, Alex and I are off to Scotland for Christmas and Hogmanay. As soon as we get back, I start school.'

'What is it?'

'Open it and see.'

Rae raised the lid and saw a tiny boat inside. She lifted it out, and placing it on the palm of her hand, she inspected the tiny model.

'It's the *Wild Spirit*!' she said with a gasp of pleasure.

'It's your Christmas present. D'you like it?' he asked shyly.

'I love it! Did you make it?'

He nodded, blushing.

And then, without thinking, she threw her arms around his neck and kissed him on the cheek.

Jamie grunted in surprise and Rae leapt back, horrified at her impulsiveness. 'I'm so sorry!' she said. 'I wasn't thinking.'

How stupid he must think her! And then another embarrassing thought occurred to her — she hadn't brought him anything for Christmas.

'Oh!' she wailed.

'What's the matter?'

'I haven't got anything to give you,' she said.

Jamie held his fingers to the place on his cheek where she'd kissed him. 'You've given me something I'll remember all over Christmas,' he said, and his face lit up with pleasure.

★ ★ ★

For once, life in the Kingsley household passed without a cross word, and Rae enjoyed Christmas far more than she'd expected. The prospect of seeing Bobby again meant she was looking forward to school, and it wouldn't be too long before the days began to lengthen and it would be the Easter holidays. She told herself she was longing to go to the harbour again and to sail in the *Wild Spirit*, but whenever she conjured up pictures in her mind's eye, it wasn't Joe she was sailing with, it was Jamie.

She'd hidden the wooden boat he'd made her away in a cupboard, although she often took it out and marvelled at how detailed the tiny model was. If Joe saw it, he'd only ridicule her and tell Mama and Papa. And then there'd be lots of teasing. No, it was best she kept it to herself.

She thought of Jamie in Scotland. Having never visited the country, she had no idea what it looked like. Other than the postcard with the lone stag on the hills which he'd sent during the summer, she could form no mental image at all, so she imagined Jamie out on those hills. It would be so long until she saw him again, and she dared not think about receiving a letter from him because if he didn't write, she'd be so disappointed.

However, the first day she returned to school, there was a letter with a Scottish stamp and postmark waiting for her. The address had been typed on a typewriter. She waited until she was alone, then tore the envelope open. Inside was a postcard. She read the message:

Wish you were here. J

She turned it over and saw the photograph of green hills reflected in what looked like a large lake. The caption said *Greetings from Loch Lomond*. On the shore of the loch were two squiggles. Rae screwed up her eyes and saw what looked like two spirals. Closer inspection showed each shape had two small lines at the front. Suddenly, she realised what they were — they were snails! Two snails crawling along with their belongings on their back.

She sat down and wrote him a long letter, drawing the same two snails at the bottom.

Several days later, she received another letter with a typewritten address, this time with an English stamp and postmark from Chichester. Inside the envelope was a postcard of the harbour near MacKenzie and Sons, and at the bottom Jamie had drawn two snails. By the time the Easter holidays arrived, she had a pile of postcards, each with two snails at the bottom.

★   ★   ★

1937

Rae's fifteenth birthday was a turning point in her life. She was another year older, but she certainly hadn't expected things to change so quickly. Nor that it would be her best friend Bobby who inadvertently brought about those changes.

Rae had begged her friend to stay with her for years, and finally Bobby had her parents' permission to go to Barlstead for a few days at the end of the Easter holidays.

'We can go sailing on the *Wild Spirit*, and you can meet my friend Jamie.'

'Is he the one who sends you those mysterious letters?'

Rae nodded. 'You'll like him. He's really good company.'

'Will Joe be there?' Bobby asked. She'd met him on several occasions and had told Rae she thought he was very handsome. 'Just like Errol Flynn,' she'd said.

To Bobby's disappointment, Joe was going to stay with a friend, but it was likely he'd be back before she returned to her parents' house in London. And at last, Bobby came to stay with her.

They'd been such good friends at school that it hadn't occurred to Rae that things would be any different at her house.

The first surprise was Bobby's

reaction to the nanny.

Rae had almost got used to Thérèse's presence at home. Jack adored her and Mama was grateful that she took over when she was working or unwell, so the household seemed to benefit from her presence. Even cranky Mrs Bolton seemed to have mellowed over the years, and there was a thinly veiled truce: Mrs Bolton only interfered with the care of Jack when the nanny wasn't there, and Thérèse didn't interfere in the kitchen at all.

When Bobby arrived at the house, Rae had briefly introduced her to Thérèse, and expected her to follow her lead and ignore the nanny. But to her surprise, her friend seemed fascinated by the young French woman. Bobby soon discovered that Thérèse's family home was not far from the house where her papa stayed when he was working in Paris, and they discussed the delights of the city like old friends.

'She's so chic!' Bobby said afterwards, 'You can't beat French women for style.'

'You can't?' asked Rae.

'Oh, no, definitely not! They have a certain *je ne sais quoi*!'

'What's that?'

'Oh, Rae, you're so funny!'

Rae joined in laughing with her friend, although she had no idea what the joke was.

'You're so lucky having Thérèse here. I bet she's wonderful to go shopping with. D'you think she knows some way we can make our uniforms look more fashionable?'

'I don't suppose so,' said Rae, who wasn't very interested in clothes. 'It's called a uniform for a reason, you know!'

'But it won't hurt to ask, will it? D'you think she's too busy to talk to us?'

And to Rae's amazement, she discovered that Thérèse was actually quite friendly.

The second surprise was Bobby's opinion of Jamie.

The two girls set off early the following morning to go sailing. She'd written to tell Jamie and he was waiting for them by the *Wild Spirit*.

'It's going to blow up this afternoon, so we've only got a couple of hours,' he said, helping Bobby aboard.

It soon became clear that Bobby was not a natural sailor. She demanded to know when they were going to arrive, and then when she realised that they were simply sailing for the fun of it, she couldn't understand why they sailed back and forth rather than going in a straight line like the cruise liners she'd been aboard. Jamie tried to explain about tacking, but she'd begun to turn pale and complain she felt sick. Reluctantly, Jamie and Rae sailed back to the harbour and helped Bobby out of the boat.

'And as for that beam swinging about!' she said crossly.

'Boom,' Jamie and Rae said together.

The girls cycled home, and by the time they reached the house, Bobby had recovered.

The following day, Jamie was waiting for them outside the boatyard.

'I wasn't sure you'd come,' he said. 'Are we sailing today?'

Rae shook her head. 'No, I thought we could show Bobby Cranston's Point.'

He looked crestfallen. 'I thought that was our . . . ' He paused and watched as Rae mounted her bicycle and set off, followed by Bobby. Then he cycled after them.

'Is this it?' Bobby asked. 'Does the tide go out or something?'

'It's only small,' said Rae, seeing it through fresh eyes.

'You can say that again!' said Bobby. 'How about we find a proper beach and get some ice creams?'

'So that's Jamie, is it?' Bobby whispered to Rae with a puzzled expression on her face. 'He's a bit immature, isn't he? I mean, you wouldn't get Errol Flynn skimming stones or Clark Gable chasing a girl with a bit of seaweed.'

In the end, Rae and Bobby cycled home early, leaving Jamie behind.

Rae had to concede that Jamie wasn't like the suave actors that she and Bobby

100

avidly watched at the cinema or whose posters hung on the walls in their shared room at St Helena's.

The following day, Mrs Bolton looked after Jack, and the girls went shopping in Chichester with Thérèse, which Rae found surprisingly enjoyable.

Now she'd turned fifteen, she was seeing the world in a different way.

I must have suddenly grown up, she thought.

* * *

The girls looked forward to their Saturday afternoon trip to the cinema all week. It wasn't seen as a 'proper' thing to do by many of the teachers, although the cinema wasn't out of bounds, so there was an added hint of defiance which made their outings even more pleasurable and exciting.

One Saturday, shortly after the Easter holidays, as they were leaving the cinema, a boy approached Bobby. 'Don't you two go to St Helena's?' he asked.

The boys went to Bishop's Hall School, which was several miles away from St Helena's. It was the school where Joe went, although Philip and Andrew were senior boys and professed not to know any of the younger pupils.

The boys offered to accompany Bobby and Rae back to school, and sitting on the seat behind the girls on the bus, Philip leaned forward to whisper in Bobby's ear, making her laugh. Andrew was more reserved. *Almost as if he's bored*, thought Rae. By the time they arrived at the bus stop near St Helena's, Philip had suggested they meet up that evening and Bobby had agreed.

When they were off the bus, Rae asked, 'You're not seriously going to meet them tonight, are you?'

'Of course!'

'But how're you going to get out of school?'

'How're *we* going to get out, you mean. I'm not sure yet. But there must be a way. Say you'll come with me!'

'I don't know.'

102

'You're not going to pass up a chance for a bit of fun, are you?'

'I'm not sure . . . '

'Come on! Let's imagine we're starring in our own film and we're off to meet two handsome heroes. It'll be such a lark!'

'Well . . . '

'Good. That's settled, then.'

Rae knew it wouldn't be possible to get out of school after the doors were locked, so there was no point arguing. They simply wouldn't be able to keep what Bobby kept referring to as their dates.

However, at bedtime Bobby put her nightdress on over her dress and told Rae to do likewise.

'We'll get into bed, and then after Miss Tansey checks us, we'll go.'

'Go where?'

'Oh, Rae! Keep up, will you! We're going to meet Philip and Andrew in the wood. And then who knows where they'll take us. Philip can drive and his father often lends him his car.'

'But how're we going to get out?' Rae was beginning to get alarmed.

'Out of the window. There's a flat roof not far below, and then it's just a short climb to the tree outside the library. I'm sure it's possible.'

'You've never done it?'

'No, of course not. But if it can be done, we're the girls to do it!'

The drop to the flat roof wasn't too far and the climb over the shallow-pitched roof of the library not too difficult, although the descent through the tree took much longer and resulted in several scratches. By keeping to the shadows, they made it to the woods on the far side of the playing fields.

'Suppose they haven't come?' Rae whispered, hoping desperately they hadn't.

'Of course, they'll come! Philip told me he'd fallen in love with me!'

Rae felt a stab of jealousy. Andrew hadn't shown any interest in her at all and she hoped that even if Philip had come, Andrew hadn't. But both boys were there.

'Drink?' said Philip, offering his hip flask to Bobby. She took a mouthful and gasped as she swallowed.

'What is it?' she asked.

'Brandy. Want some more?' He drank some, then passed her the flask again, and she took another mouthful and wiped her mouth with the back of her hand like he'd done.

'Here,' said Andrew, passing his hip flask to Rae. She took it and allowed the liquid to touch her lips, but it burned and she returned the flask to him.

'No, thanks.'

'Please yourself,' he said, and took several gulps.

'Come for a walk with me,' he said, and took Rae's hand. She reluctantly followed with a backward glance at Bobby, but to her surprise, she and Philip were kissing, just like she'd seen in the Holly-wood films. Except it wasn't exactly like in the movies, because somehow that seemed glamorous and charming. The hero and heroine were usually in elegant surroundings and everything was perfect. This seemed to be . . . well, rather grubby, thought Rae.

This isn't what I was expecting at all.

Andrew pulled her towards him and held his arms tightly around her waist, then lowered his mouth to hers. It took her by surprise, and she stood frozen for a second, but that was enough for him to place his brandy-flavoured lips on hers.

So this is what it's like to be kissed.

Rae wondered what all the fuss was about. It wasn't very nice, and if this was kissing, she wasn't planning to do it again any time soon. Then Andrew pulled her down to the ground, but as he did so, his hand went up her skirt. She shoved it away, thinking he hadn't realised where his hand had gone, but when he roughly pushed it back and tried to hold her down, she began to panic. This wasn't how Clark Gable behaved! She brought her knee up to his stomach and as he grunted in pain, she leapt up and backed away.

'Bobby!' she called as loudly as she dared, and stumbled to where she'd last seen her friend and Philip. But he was lying on top of her, and when Bobby saw her, she angrily waved her hand in a gesture of dismissal.

Rae ran. She climbed the tree, back onto the library roof, and then realised that although the drop from the window to the flat roof wasn't far and she could just touch the window sill, she didn't have the strength in her arms to climb back on her own. She sank down onto the roof and waited for Bobby to return so that they could get back in together. The cuts and scratches she'd acquired during her frantic scramble up through the tree now throbbed and stung, although they weren't very painful. Certainly not painful enough to make her cry. So she didn't know why she'd started sobbing, but once she'd started, she carried on until there were no more tears.

Bobby returned shortly after, and by linking her hands together for Rae to step on, they both managed to get back into the bedroom.

After that, Rae refused any more night-time sorties with Bobby, who declared she would do whatever it took to be with Philip, because as she said, 'We love each other passionately.'

Each night Rae helped Bobby to climb back into their bedroom, but the friendship and closeness they'd developed seemed to have gone.

Several weeks after they'd first met the boys outside the cinema, Rae awoke to hear muffled sobs from Bobby's bed.

'Bobby? Bobby! What's wrong?'

'Oh, Rae! I don't know what to do! I'm late.'

Rae looked at her clock. 'No, Bobby. There's still half an hour before we need to get up. I think you've had a nightmare.'

Bobby gripped her wrist. 'I mean I haven't had —'

'What? What haven't you had? Bobby, you're frightening me! You're not making any sense.'

Bobby buried her face in her hands. 'Rae, I think I'm pregnant!'

The only time Rae had heard the word *pregnant* before was when Mrs Bolton's dog had had a litter of pups. Bobby was obviously confused and had used the wrong word.

'Bobby, what d'you mean?'

'Rae,' she wailed, 'For goodness sake! Don't you understand? I'm going to have a baby!'

'Don't be ridiculous, Bobby! You can't be! You're not married!'

'Oh, Rae, you're such a child! You don't have to be married to have a baby!'

Rae was certain you *did* have to be married to have a baby. She didn't know of anyone who was still single with a child, but she didn't want to upset Bobby further. 'Well,' she said gently, 'how can it be possible, then?'

'Because . . . ' Bobby sobbed. 'Because . . . Philip and I we . . . well, we kissed . . . and things.'

Rae knew Bobby was mistaken. It

couldn't possibly be true. 'Shall I get Nurse?' she asked finally.

Bobby nodded. 'Just tell her I feel ill, won't you? I don't want her to know. It's going to be bad enough telling my parents. Papa's going to have a fit.'

Her parents came the following day and took Bobby away after an interview with the headmistress. She was allowed to pack her things and say goodbye to Rae.

'I'm sorry, I had to tell them you helped me back into the room each evening,' she said. 'But I didn't tell them about you meeting Andrew. Just keep quiet and they'll never know. Stick to the story. I'll write when I can. Now promise me you won't tell them about Andrew.'

'All right, although I don't want to lie.'

'Just do it, Rae.'

Rae was called to the headmistress's office and was horrified to see both her parents there.

Miss Frost asked for her side of the story, and Rae told how she'd helped Bobby back into the room each evening but omitted her part in the first outing. She felt deceitful, but it would only have made it worse for Bobby because it would show that she'd lied. Although Rae wasn't sure how it could possibly be worse for Bobby.

'So,' Miss Frost said, 'I feel that under the circumstances, it might be best if Hannah-Rae goes home immediately and doesn't return this term. She has abused my trust by not coming to me and telling me about Roberta's scandalous behaviour. Had she done so, a disaster might have been avoided.'

The trip home had been silent, but Rae knew that once the shock had worn off, she would be in serious trouble. She felt sick with shame. Being sent home from school and not being allowed back until September, as well as the guilt of knowing she'd lied to everyone about meeting Andrew!

And it had all been for what? It wasn't as if she'd wanted to meet him, and it certainly wasn't as if she'd enjoyed it.

There was no shouting when they

arrived home. Mama went to bed without saying anything, and Papa looked at her with such disappointment that it nearly broke her heart. What would they think if they knew she'd gone with Bobby that first time and met Andrew?

She was suddenly gripped with a terrible thought. Bobby had said she was going to have a baby because she'd been with Philip, and . . . what was it she'd said? *Kissed and things.*

Andrew had kissed her! True, it hadn't lasted very long. But how long did it take? Why hadn't she known about being pregnant and kissing and things? And, anyway, what were *things*?

Suppose she was pregnant? How would she know? What should she do? One thing was certain, she couldn't ask Mama or Papa.

There was only one other adult in the house — Mrs Bolton. Should she ask her? No, she'd be sure to tell her parents.

Rae lay awake most of the night, crying and fretting about what would happen if suddenly a baby burst out of her. Everyone would know and her disgrace would be complete.

In the morning when she finally got up, Mama had taken Jack to the doctor's surgery in the village, Papa had gone to work, and Mrs Bolton was in the kitchen humming tunelessly. During the night, Rae had remembered Thérèse. She'd got so used to ignoring the French girl, she hadn't considered asking her, but she was much older than Rae and might have the information she needed. And there was no one else. Rae decided she would tell Thérèse she had a friend with a problem, which was true, and just say that her friend didn't know what to do and that she needed some help.

She got as far as Thérèse's door three times before she summoned the courage to knock. If she didn't hurry up soon, Mama would be back and the opportunity would be lost.

Rae took a deep breath and tapped on the door to Thérèse's room.

113

'Come in.'

Thérèse was sitting in front of her dressing table, combing her hair and arranging the kiss curls she wore on either side of her face and on her forehead. She gasped when she saw Rae's swollen eyes and blotchy face. 'Are you unwell?'

'No, I don't think so.' Then remembering she was supposed to be asking for information for a friend, she said, 'I hope I'm not disturbing you, but I have a friend and she's in trouble . . . well, she might be in trouble . . . and I really want to help, but . . .'

It didn't take long for Thérèse to work out what was really bothering Rae. 'Now, *chérie*, you must tell me everything, down to the tiniest detail. Don't be afraid, I won't judge you.'

Rae poured out the whole story of that first meeting with Andrew and Philip.

'And you say he just kissed you and

then tried to pull you onto the ground?'

Rae hung her head and nodded.

'And he tried to put his hand up your skirt but you kneed him and then he stopped?'

She nodded again, tears streaming down her face.

Thérèse got up and put her arm around Rae's shoulders. 'There's nothing to cry about, *chérie*. I can assure you if you've been honest with me, there is no possibility of you being pregnant.'

'Are you sure?'

'*Certainement!* Most certainly!'

Rae sank on to Thérèse's bed and sobbed with relief.

'Your mother didn't tell you about how babies are made?' Thérèse asked in disbelief.

'No.'

'That is shameful!' Thérèse said angrily. 'Then I will tell you all you need to know. But I warn you, you may be shocked. Do you want me to carry on?'

'Please, Thérèse. I would very much like you to tell me.'

★ ★ ★

What shocked Rae most was that she'd been living in a world where, despite believing she was so grown up, so many things had been happening to the adults around her, about which she'd known nothing. She'd been aware of the girls at school whispering about things but she'd deliberately not wanted to find out.

Why had the word *pregnant*, for example, only come to her attention once, when Mrs Bolton had mentioned it regarding her dog? How had she not known the risk she'd put herself in by going out with Bobby that evening to meet those two boys? Had Bobby known how foolishly she'd behaved? She'd always described herself as worldly wise, but Rae suspected that her wisdom about the world hadn't been quite as complete as she'd thought.

At the end of the long explanation,

which appeared to take in all sorts of surprising things — marriage, men and women's bodies, where babies grew, how to avoid having babies, to name a few — Thérèse put her hand on Rae's.

'That's a lot to take in, *chérie*. I'm very angry your mother didn't tell you all of these things gradually, or even a few of these things. But I think perhaps she hasn't realised how fast you're growing up. This is something you wouldn't tell a young child. She may not have realised you're ready to know.'

Rae simply nodded and thanked Thérèse; there was so much swirling around in her mind, it was hard to think what to say. All those Hollywood movies that she and Bobby had ardently devoured, imagining it was they who swept into a room in glamorous gowns, danced on a moonlit lawn, were serenaded beneath their bedroom window, had all been make-believe and hadn't reflected real life at all. When the hero had presented his lady with an enormous bouquet of red roses and sung to her, that hadn't been the end of the matter; they'd finally taken off all their clothes and . . . Rae shook her head in disbelief. It wasn't romantic at all! It was revolting.

She wanted to get away to think and to absorb all she'd learned. Stealing into the kitchen while Mrs Bolton was in the garden hanging out washing, Rae took a few apples and two of the biscuits that were cooling on the rack, then quietly wheeling her bicycle across the lawn, so it didn't crunch on the gravel of the drive, she climbed on and started to pedal. There was no plan in her mind, other than to ride until she was exhausted. But at the crossroads, she turned towards the harbour. Perhaps she'd go and sit on *Wild Spirit* and stare at the water while she tried to make some sense of what Thérèse had told her, and of the betrayal she felt at her parents' lack of guidance.

When she reached the boat, she had the urge to rig her and sail away. She wouldn't, of course, because she recognised that as a fanciful romantic notion.

Something someone in a Hollywood movie might do. But today the world was a harsher, bleaker place. She longed for yesterday when things were simpler, when all she had to worry about were the tides and the weather forecast for a day of sailing.

She knew Jamie would be in his father's boatyard, working. He'd wanted to go to college, but his father had insisted that if he was to run the boatyard one day with his brother Alex, they both needed to know how to do everything, from the lowest jobs to the highest.

She wondered what he'd be doing today, and suddenly she longed to see him, to check that he was still the same.

School had changed.

Home had changed.

Bobby had changed.

But surely her friendship with Jamie wouldn't have been touched? Yes, she needed to see Jamie. She needed some reassurance that the entire universe hadn't gone mad.

But she couldn't wait at the harbour

and simply hope he'd come out of the yard. He might not appear for hours, and then he'd undoubtedly come out with his father and there would be no chance to talk to him alone. If she wanted to see him, she'd simply have to go in and ask for him. But as she neared the gate and heard several of the men calling to each other, she wondered if perhaps it would be better to hover by the gate and hope Jamie saw her.

''Ello, love — waitin' for me, are you?' one of the men called good-naturedly when he saw Rae at the gate.

'I was hoping to talk to Jamie, please,' she said, aware that her cheeks were flaming.

'Jamie,' he yelled, 'there's a lovely young lady waitin' for you!'

When there was no response, an unseen voice called out, 'Jamie! That Susannah's waitin' for you! Get a move on!'

'It ain't Susannah!' the first man yelled. 'It's another young lady!'

There was a chorus of 'Oooooh!'

from several of the others, and finally Jamie appeared at the gate.

'Rae! What're you doing here? Have you broken up already?'

'Oooooh! It's Rae!' one of the men shouted, and they all laughed.

'Let's go down to the harbour,' Jamie said with an embarrassed smile.

He seemed taller and broader than when Rae had last seen him; less like the boy she remembered.

'So come on, tell me! What're you doing here?' he asked.

'I . . . I . . . ' Rae didn't know where to begin. 'D'you think we can go to Cranston's Point?'

He looked back over his shoulder at the yard. 'I can't leave yet, but as soon as I can, I'll get away. Can you wait for me?'

She nodded.

Rae sat on the harbour wall, dangling her legs over, and watched *Wild Spirit* rock gently on the water until Jamie appeared with his bicycle, and they set off.

She remembered the last time they'd been to the beach with Bobby and how it had seemed so dull. Would it be the magical place it once had been, or would it, too, be spoiled?

They leaned their bicycles against the ruins and Jamie led the way to their large rock and sat down. He remained silent, waiting for her to speak, then as she began to cry, he put his arm around her shoulders and pulled her close. It was quite unexpected but strangely comforting. Certainly not the sort of thing he'd ever done before.

She started hesitantly at first, telling him she'd been sent home from school in disgrace until the end of the summer term.

'So you're back until September?' he asked.

'Yes.'

'That's good,' he said.

'Don't you want to know why?'

'D'you want to tell me?'

She told him about how she'd helped Bobby get back in through the window and that she was now expecting a baby and had been removed from school by her parents.

'I'm not surprised,' he said. 'She seemed a bit of a flirt.'

Rae was astonished. 'What makes you say that?'

'Because when she came, she was fluttering her eyelashes at my brother. He told me.'

'I don't think she was flirting! She was trying to look like Jean Harlow. She practised in the mirror. She didn't mean any harm.'

Jamie didn't seem convinced. 'I think anyone who sneaks out of school to meet a boy in the woods is asking for trouble,' he said.

'Oh!' Rae wailed.

'I'm really sorry you've lost a friend,' he said, 'but it wasn't fair of her to get you mixed up in it so you got punished too. But perhaps you'll be able to come down to the harbour more often now. When I finish work tomorrow, we could take *Wild Spirit* out. What d'you think?

Or we could come here. I'll try to get off early . . . ' He pulled her closer and put his other arm around her, his face now inches from hers.

What was he doing? Rae wanted a friend, not someone who pulled her about like Andrew had done. She pushed him away.

'So anyone who sneaks out of school to meet a boy is asking for trouble, is she?' she demanded angrily. And then, unable to stop herself, she added, 'Well, I'll have you know, I wasn't asking for trouble when I went with Bobby!'

His mouth opened but no sound came out. Finally, he whispered, 'What are you saying?'

'I'm saying the first time Bobby went out, I was with her. And I met a boy called Andrew. And he kissed me and it was horrible. And I never want to kiss anyone ever again. *Ever!*'

She turned and ran back to her bicycle, then climbing on, she pedalled as fast as she could away from Cranston's Point . . . and Jamie.

2

How could things have gone so spectacularly wrong? Jamie wondered.

He watched the wavelets lapping the sand along the tiny strip of beach which had once been his favourite place in the whole world. It had been their secret place, his and Rae's. It was so small that no one bothered to visit it when there were so many other beaches not far away, and so every time they'd cycled to it, they'd been alone; well, until the day Rae had suggested that dreadful girl, Bobby, join them. He hadn't been able to believe that after the girl had sneered at the *Wild Spirit* and at sailing in general, Rae had wanted to take her to their private place, Cranston's Point.

Bobby had scoffed at their beach and Rae had seemed to agree with her. That had hurt, but not as much as when he overheard Bobby criticising him for being childish. He hadn't reacted to her comments but he'd expected Rae to disagree and to stand up for him. She hadn't, and that had stung more than anything. Rae was turning into a different person thanks to Bobby.

Rae obviously thought he was childish.

He might not be a man, but he was nearly as strong as any of the men who worked in his father's yard. He knew deep down Bobby hadn't been referring to his strength, although exactly what she had meant, he wasn't sure. And more importantly, he had no idea what to do about it, if indeed anything could be done.

After Rae and Bobby left, Jamie found his father in the office.

'Am I childish, Dad?'

Mr MacKenzie removed the pipe from his mouth and considered the question for a second. 'Is that what the Kingsley lassie said?' he asked finally.

'No. But her friend said it.'

Mr MacKenzie nodded. 'I know you

like Rae, son, but she's not a suitable friend for you.'

'But it wasn't Rae who said it, it was Bobby.'

'And did Rae stand up for you?'

'Well, no . . . '

'Best forget her, lad. She's too wayward. And she's not of our class. Sooner or later, your friendship would've ended. Looks like it's sooner. And I can see you're upset. But believe me, son, it's for the best.'

Jamie had walked out of the office then and cycled back to the cottage where he lived with his father and brother, Alex. He'd asked Dad a question about himself and received an answer about Rae being an unsuitable friend. How had that helped him? But it wasn't surprising. He knew his father didn't like Rae.

Jamie recalled the day he'd first set eyes on her. He could still remember how wonderful she'd looked in her pink coat and hat. Never before had he seen anything so beautiful, and he'd stared at her in adoration. But he'd even got that wrong, because for some reason, he'd upset her. It'd seemed so unjust; he couldn't believe she didn't know how much he admired her.

Why hadn't she been able to see? But he'd obviously done something wrong because her response had been to poke her tongue out at him. To his shame, in embarrassment and confusion, he'd pushed her. Of course, he hadn't actually intended to knock her to the ground — that hadn't been his wish at all. It was simply an attempt to make her realise she'd been behaving unfairly. But once she got up, she was furious . . . and then came the punch.

Dad had never forgiven her for that. 'They let that Kingsley lassie run wild,' he'd say whenever Rae's name came up, until Jamie didn't mention her at all unless it was unavoidable, because the truth was, he thought she was magnificent and he longed to spend time with her despite his dad's misgivings. What was more, he was awash with feelings for her which he couldn't pin down. He didn't even have the words to describe them.

But there must be words for how he felt. Someone must be able to explain it to him. If his mother was still alive, he would've asked her, although he had no idea if she'd have sided with his father and taken a dislike to Rae.

But he and Alex had been without a mother for many years, and although he knew his brother still retained memories of her, he had none. How had Alex managed to navigate through feelings such as he had for Rae? Or perhaps his brother didn't have such complicated emotions, and it was simply that there was something odd about him.

During the next few days, he listened carefully to conversations between the men who worked in his father's boatyard. Two of the younger ones were about to get married and Jamie eavesdropped, taking note of comments that he wouldn't have noticed before. Much of it didn't make sense, but he began to get the picture that girls liked a man who was decisive, a leader, and one who told them what to do. He wasn't sure Rae would be one of those girls. He wondered if his father had treated his mother like that.

'Dad,' he said one day when they were alone, 'did Mum like it if you always told her what to do?'

'No, son. No one always likes to be told what to do by someone else. Who's been filling your head with nonsense?'

'Oh, it's just something I overheard.'

'That wouldn't be young Arthur and Pete, would it?'

'Well . . . '

'I should take whatever those lads say with a pinch o' salt.'

And that had been that.

And then Susannah Turner had started to take an interest in him. She was two years younger and still attended the school where he'd once gone, but she passed the boatyard every day and always loitered by the gate so she could wave to him. She was pretty enough, but she didn't compare to Rae in Jamie's eyes.

One day his father and Alex went to Chichester for the afternoon, leaving Jamie to walk home on his own after work. Susannah was waiting for him and said that she was going his way, so she'd walk with him. She'd taken his arm and he'd been too embarrassed to push her away; it seemed unkind. And then she'd suggested a shortcut through the woods. There was no shortcut as far as he knew, but she insisted, and again, he didn't want to hurt her feelings so he followed her. She led him into the undergrowth and kissed him on the lips, which had taken him by surprise. So much so that he forgot to worry about offending her and pushed her away. Then with flaming cheeks, he continued his walk home. Susannah had run after him, and to his amazement, seemed even keener on him than ever.

Perhaps Arthur and Pete were right: girls liked to know who was boss.

The afternoon Rae was waiting for

131

him in the harbour café, he'd had some sort of strategy worked out. Not that he'd expected to see her again before the start of the summer holidays, but he knew she'd be back, even if only to sail *Wild Spirit*.

She'd seemed troubled about something, so he'd suggested they go to their private beach. There was no point wasting time; he'd put his arm around her like Arthur had told Pete he'd done when he'd first met his girl, and it crossed his mind he might even kiss her when she'd told him why she was home so early from school. He had a rough idea what to do from Susannah's attempt to kiss him.

But Rae took him completely by surprise when she told him why she'd been sent home from school. And when she said she'd kissed that boy, he'd felt a stab of jealousy so intense he'd almost doubled up.

She'd looked at him as if waiting for him to say something, but what *could* he say? He just stared at her. Stupidly.

Then she'd said she never wanted to kiss anyone again, and she'd gone.

And now he was alone on their rock, on their beach once again. He'd got it wrong.

On his way home, he decided to go to Rae's house the following day and apologise. What he'd be apologising for, he didn't know, but that wouldn't stop him. He'd admit to anything if Rae would smile at him again and if they could be friends.

When Jamie got home, Alex was working in the vegetable plot.

'Alex, have you ever had feelings for a girl?' he blurted out.

His brother looked up in surprise. 'None of your business,' he said sharply, and carried on digging.

'But Alex! There are things I need to know and I've no idea who to ask.'

Alex was silent for a while, then he said, 'D'you remember Aunt Lily?'

'Mum's sister?'

'Yes.'

Jamie nodded. He remembered her,

133

although he hadn't seen her for several years. There had been some sort of argument between her and his father and all visits to her had stopped.

'Go and see her,' Alex said. 'She'll sort you out. But don't tell Dad you've been. Nor that I told you to go.'

* * *

'Jamie! How lovely to see you!' Aunt Lily said when she opened the door to her cottage. 'Come in, come in!'

She invited Jamie into the parlour, and once she'd made sure he was comfortable, she busied herself in the kitchen making tea. He looked about the room and was surprised at how different it was from his home, which was plain, drab and often very untidy. In his aunt's house, everything was neat; there were embroidered cushions on the chairs and lace runners on the sideboard and the small tables, all of which were covered in china ornaments and photograph frames. He glanced at the one closest to him; it showed two young girls sitting on a furry rug in a photographer's studio. It was obvious from the similarity in their features that they were sisters. In fact, they could have been twins, although one of the girls appeared to be slightly younger than the other. He looked at the other photographs and saw that mostly they featured the two girls at different stages of life; and as they approached adulthood, he could see that the slightly taller one was his aunt. That, of course, meant the other girl was his mother. He swallowed hard and tears came to his eyes. There were no photographs of Mum in his father's house; no memories of her at all — well, none that were obvious to him, anyway.

Standing on the mantelpiece was a wedding photograph, and for a second he thought his aunt was the bride, which was strange because he'd never heard that he had an uncle. Then he realised the bridesmaid was slightly taller than the bride. It was his parents' wedding, and the bridesmaid was Aunt Lily. How happy everyone appeared; how young and hopeful his parents looked.

'I love that photograph,' Aunt Lily said, returning with a tray on which she had a fancy teapot and delicate cups and saucers. 'It was such a wonderful day.'

'We don't have any photographs like that,' said Jamie.

Aunt Lily nodded, her eyes downcast. 'That's a shame, son. A real shame. But I suspected as much. Your father couldn't bear anything to remind him of your mother after she'd passed away — not even me, in the end.'

'Is that why we don't see you anymore?'

She nodded and bit her lip as if fighting back tears, then busied herself pouring tea. By the time she'd finished, she'd composed herself. 'Now, to what do I owe the pleasure of your visit?'

He stared at her for a moment. 'I'm not sure where to begin, Aunt . . .'

'I always find the beginning is the best place to start,' she said, and smiled encouragingly. 'I've got a pot of stew cooking and there's plenty for two, so we have as much time as you need.'

When Jamie finished explaining about Rae, and how he'd tried to be what he thought she wanted, and how upset she'd been when he'd pulled her to him, she nodded sympathetically.

'Everyone treats me like a child,' Jamie said, 'and no one'll talk to me about anything, so how can I ever learn? All Dad wants to do is warn me off Rae. Alex seems too embarrassed to say anything, and the men in the yard just laugh at me.'

'Ah,' she said, nodding her head again, 'men can sometimes be rather bad at expressing their feelings.'

'So how do men know what they're supposed to do when they grow up?'

'How indeed?' she said. 'But actually, Jamie, I think you'll find that many of them don't. They are the men who bottle everything up and never discuss things. Those like you who want to understand about their feelings and how others think usually do very well in love and in their lives in general.'

'Do you think that I . . . ?' Jamie hesitated.

'Yes?'

'Well, d'you think I could be in love?' Jamie asked. He blushed.

'It's not possible for me to say, Jamie. Only you would know.'

'But how *would* I know?'

'Hmm, that's a hard one.' She sighed. 'Everyone is different, but in my experience, you know you love someone when they're the first person you think about when you wake up in the morning and the last person on your mind when you go to sleep at night. When you find that things are meaningless unless you're sharing them with that person, and when you feel as if you're half alive when they're not there.'

'That's how I feel about Rae,' Jamie whispered. 'But isn't being in love supposed to be happy? I feel miserable.

138

Rae was so upset with me that I'm not sure she'll ever speak to me again. I can't tell Dad about how I feel because he doesn't like her, and if I tell everyone else, they'll just laugh and say I'm too young to know what I'm talking about.'

'The best thing is not to tell anyone else; it isn't their business. But it would be a good idea to talk to Rae and find out how she feels. That won't be an easy conversation because she may not share your feelings. Remember, she's younger than you, although girls do mature earlier than boys. But if you're ever going to have peace of mind, it's a discussion you need to have. But don't ever let anyone tell you you're too young to fall in love and that it won't last. I fell in love when I was about your age. He didn't feel the same about me and he married someone else. But I still love him. I always will.' Her eyes filled with tears and she looked towards the wedding photograph on the mantel-piece.

Surely she couldn't mean she loved Dad? Was that why they'd all stopped visiting Aunt Lily? Jamie wasn't sure if he should say something or pretend he hadn't noticed her tears. But if it was Dad she loved, how terrible for her, because once Dad made up his mind about something, he was very hard to shift. They must both once have shared a love for his mother; surely they could have consoled each other and made each other happy?

Finally, Aunt Lily dabbed her eyes with a handkerchief and suggested they have supper. Jamie helped her to set the table.

'Your father has raised you to be a polite young man, Jamie. Your mother would be so proud. You know, you said you were worried about how to behave with girls, but I think it's inside you already. Forget all the things you've heard in the boatyard about women liking a strong, bossy man. I think you'll find that women like a man who makes them feel like they're the most precious person in the world and lets them know they're appreciated and respected. If you keep that uppermost in your mind, you won't go far wrong.'

* * *

Dad was reading his newspaper in the parlour when Jamie got home that evening.

'Been out, laddie?'

'Yes, Dad.'

'Have you been with the Kingsley lass?'

'No!' he said crossly. And then although he hadn't intended to tell his father, he added, 'I've been with Aunt Lily.'

'Oh!'

Jamie had expected anger; in fact, there was nothing he'd have liked more than an argument with his father for always being so set against Rae. But Dad's gasp had not been angry, and Jamie saw that when he laid his pipe in the ashtray, his hand was shaking.

141

'And how is your aunt?' he asked in a strained voice.

'Fine. Although I think she's lonely.'

'Did she say so?'

'No, but I could tell.'

'She's living alone, then?'

'Yes . . . Dad?'

'Yes?'

'Why doesn't she come here now? She used to come, I remember.'

His father sighed. 'Some things are just better left unsaid. Now, you'd better get off to bed.'

The following morning, Jamie got up very early and cycled to Rae's house in Barlstead. He'd be late for work but he'd just have to put up with his father's anger. With any luck, he could apologise and be back at work before his father noticed. But he doubted it. Nevertheless, it would be worth it.

Jamie had never been inside Rae's house, although on two occasions he'd been with his father when he'd dropped something off to Dr Kingsley, so he rode straight to it and stopped outside the gate to smooth his hair back into place and to give him a few moments to gather his thoughts.

He'd tried to rehearse a speech but nothing sounded right, and he hoped that if Rae gave him the opportunity, the right words would come. Leaning his bicycle against the gate, he walked up the gravel drive. Well, Dad was right about one thing — the Kingsleys were much wealthier than his family. But did that matter?

He took a deep breath and knocked on the door.

A stout woman who was drying her hands on her apron opened it. 'Yes?'

'Please would it be possible to see Rae?' he asked, assuming this must be Mrs Bolton.

'I'm afraid she's not here.'

'When will she be back?'

'I've no idea. Possibly August. I don't know. No one tells me anything.'

'August?' Was Mrs Bolton joking?

'Yes, she's staying with relatives.'

'Do you have an address?'

'No, sorry.' She turned and began to shut the door.

'Please!' he said in desperation.

'I told you, I don't have an address.' She closed the door firmly.

Rae had gone. It wasn't possible!

As he walked slowly down the drive, the door opened and he turned back to see if Mrs Bolton had suddenly remembered where Rae had gone. But it wasn't the housekeeper, it was a very smart young woman who beckoned him.

'You are Jamie MacKenzie?' she asked in her gentle French accent.

'Yes.'

'Ah!' She seemed to be assessing him. 'Well, Jamie MacKenzie, although Mrs Bolton doesn't know where Rae has gone, luckily for you, I do.' She handed him a slip of paper. Then with a smile, she closed the door.

3

'Is there someone at the door?' Mrs Bolton called from the kitchen.

'No,' said Thérèse. She smiled to herself as she climbed the stairs to continue her packing. The letter from Lady Langton accepting her application for the post of nanny lay on her bedside table and Thérèse read it once again. The chauffeur would arrive tomorrow to pick her up and take her to Lady Langton's residence in London.

Joe was at school. Rae was at this moment being driven to relatives somewhere in Essex, and when Thérèse sat down to dinner with Dr and Mrs Kingsley later that evening, Jack would be in bed. Then the fireworks would begin!

Of course, she ought to work her notice, but she suspected that after she told them about her new post at dinner that evening and then made her speech, Mrs Kingsley would be so furious, she'd be glad to see Thérèse go immediately.

She would miss Jack, who was a delightful boy, but now he was at school and had lots of friends, she barely saw him, so there was no point her staying with the Kingsleys. And the fact that Mrs Kingsley now expected her to do housework and other chores when Jack wasn't there really upset her. She looked down at her perfect almond-shaped nails. These were not the hands of a woman who washed floors and cleaned silver. No, it was time to go. In fact, if anything, she'd stayed too long; but until Jack had begun school, he'd been quite clingy. Not surprising, of course, with a mother like that! Why did she find it so hard to make her children feel wanted? Joe seemed to be the least affected by his mother's coldness, but he was so charming that somehow he managed to get through to his mother and find a place in her affection.

As for Rae and Jack, they both needed to feel their mother's love, but although Thérèse didn't doubt Mrs Kingsley adored all her children, she seemed to have difficulty in showing it. And now she'd sent Rae away to stay with her cousin, Thérèse knew that the girl would be suffering. As if she hadn't been through enough! But what did her mother know of that? Very little.

If she'd prepared her daughter better, the incident with Bobby could've been avoided. But tonight, it would be Thérèse's chance to air her views and to tell a few — as the British said — home truths.

The following day, Lady Langton's chauffeur arrived and loaded Thérèse's luggage into the car. Dr Kingsley had gone to work, Jack was at school, and Mrs Kingsley was in her bedroom with a headache, so only Mrs Bolton waited on the doorstep to wave her a half-hearted goodbye. They'd never got on, although they'd established a truce.

So that's it, thought Thérèse. *Mrs*

Kingsley can't even be bothered to say goodbye. Although to be fair, Thérèse had not spared her feelings last night and had been scathing of her employer's mothering skills to the extent that she had been reduced to tears.

Good! thought Thérèse. *Rae and Jack are too young and inexperienced to stand up for themselves.*

'So I hear you're French,' said the chauffeur. 'Where're you from?'

'Paris,' said Thérèse, looking out of the window.

It wouldn't do to encourage him. She had her sights on a richer husband than this man. When she'd first come to stay with the Kingsleys, she'd imagined the house would be full of doctors and other important people from London hospitals. But the social life had been very poor in such a small village. Still, she was on her way to London now and things were going to be different.

4

While Rae had been out with Jamie, her parents had discussed how they were going to punish her and what was to happen to her until the new school year.

'I simply can't cope with any more of your thoughtless impulsiveness,' Mama had told Rae when she reached home, 'so I've arranged for you to stay with my cousin Joanna and her family.'

If Rae hadn't been so upset after seeing Jamie, she might have fought harder to stay at home, but she was numb. It was as if her life were a kaleidoscope. As soon as she started to get used to a particular pattern and its colours, someone rotated the cylinder, sending all the shapes tumbling into new positions. Without Bobby, school would be different. Now that Mama was studying, home was different. Even

Jamie had changed. Perhaps it was a good thing she was being sent to Joanna's. But deep inside, it didn't feel like a good thing. Being sent away was never a good thing.

Mama had driven her to Joanna's early the following morning and the journey passed in silence. What was there to say? Rae was fighting back tears and Mama complained she had a nervous headache, which although she didn't say, Rae felt sure was being blamed on her.

Joanna and four-year-old Faye were waiting at the door of Priory Hall to welcome them, but after a cup of tea and an inspection of Joanna's newborn son Mark, Mama said she was sure she had a migraine coming and thought it best she get home as quickly as she could.

'Your poor mother,' said Joanna. 'Well, let's get you settled in, shall we? And then I'll show you around. Hopefully Mark won't wake for a while.'

It seemed that Joanna was aware of

Rae's exclusion from school, and having observed Mama's frostiness with her usual calm patience, she set about making Rae feel at home.

Joanna's husband Ben was a solicitor who worked in his father's company in the small town of Laindon, which was a few miles away, although he'd inherited Priory Hall and its farmland. But he, too, was kind and welcomed their new guest. It was obvious that he adored Joanna and his children, and although Rae knew her father loved Mama, she wondered why their house had never been as peaceful. But then, thought Rae, although Joanna and Mama were first cousins, they were not alike at all.

Rae wasn't sure exactly what her position was in the household, so she tried to help out as best she could, and one day while she was helping the cook, she was sent out to pick peas. The vegetable garden needed tidying, and after dinner she set to, hoeing and weeding — a job which obviously hadn't been done for some time. Joanna had been very grateful when she'd looked out of Mark's bedroom window. He had colic, slept very little and needed a lot of attention.

'I love working in the garden,' Rae said. 'Perhaps I could work out there tomorrow.'

Rae preferred to be outdoors, and when she'd finished in the vegetable garden, she sorted out the cottage garden, bringing that under control. Days passed and she realised she wasn't looking forward to going home, or back to school. But how long had Mama arranged for her to stay at Priory Hall? She dared not ask in case she reminded someone that she was just a guest and that ultimately she would have to go home. And she dreaded Mama arriving in the car ready to take her away.

A rather fat envelope had arrived a fortnight before, addressed in her mother's handwriting, and Rae had opened it nervously, hoping it wouldn't be a summons home. However, inside was a letter from Bobby in Switzerland, who was unaware of Rae's current address. There was no mention of the baby, and Rae began to wonder if there had been no pregnancy after all. Perhaps Bobby really was less worldly wise than she believed herself to be. Apparently she was staying with friends of her parents in their chalet and going on some glorious mountain walks. Thérèse had said it was likely that Bobby's parents would send her away. Once the baby was born, they would find it a family and then bring their daughter home. It seemed monstrous to give a child away, but perhaps, Rae thought, it was better to be somewhere where you were happy than with a mother who didn't want you.

Bobby's letter had been disturbing because of all the things that hadn't been said about the baby, but at least Mama's brief letter which had also been in the envelope hadn't requested she return to Barlstead.

Two weeks later, at breakfast time, however, Joanna told Rae there was a letter for her on the hall table. She went out into the garden to start work, deliberately ignoring it. If it was another redirected letter from Bobby, asking why she hadn't replied, she'd simply feel guilty, and if it was from her mother telling her to pack her bags, she didn't want to know.

Joanna found her hoeing the lines of vegetables and asked her if she would mind working in her mother-in-law's garden about a mile away from Priory Hall, and Rae accepted gladly.

'If you find her a bit . . . well, difficult, I shan't blame you for refusing to go there,' Joanna had said. 'She can be very . . . ' She sighed. ' . . . cantankerous. And very hard to please. Oh, and don't forget, there's a letter on the hall table for you.'

Rae had been rather nervous about Joanna's mother-in-law, but she told herself if she could stand up to Mama, she could probably withstand Mrs Richardson's displeasure. After all, she could simply put her tools back in the shed and walk off.

She decided to set off immediately and try to forget about the letter waiting for her on the hall table. She'd enjoy the sunshine and hopefully Mrs Richardson would ignore her.

She'd just started down the drive when Joanna called after her, 'Rae, I've packed you lunch. I don't know if my mother-in-law will make you anything, and I don't want you starving all day — assuming you last the day!' She walked down the drive to Rae and handed her the small parcel of food and the letter. 'Here, darling; you keep forgetting your letter. I didn't know you knew anyone in Southend.'

Rae looked at the postmark — Southend-on-Sea. The handwriting definitely wasn't Mama's, Papa's, or anyone else's that she knew. Sliding her finger under the flap, she opened the envelope and took out the letter.

'Is everything all right, darling?' Joanna asked.

'Yes, thank you, Joanna. It's just from

someone I once knew. A friend. Nothing interesting.'

Joanna went back into the house and Rae continued to look at the name at the bottom of the letter — Jamie MacKenzie.

Dear Rae,

I hope you are well. The day after I last saw you, I went to your house but you'd already left with your mother. The nanny gave me your address. I hope you don't mind me writing to you.

I am now working at my uncle's boatyard in Leigh-on-Sea while he recovers from a fall.

I believe I angered you the last time we met and I would like the chance to apologise to you, and if possible, to become friends again.

I will be free this Wednesday afternoon and I will be arriving at Laindon Station on the train shortly after noon. If you would be willing to see me so that I can apologise, perhaps we can meet outside Baxter's Tea Rooms. I

*will be there from one o'clock and
I will wait until three o'clock.*

*I understand if you do not want to
meet me.*

*Yours sincerely,
Jamie MacKenzie.*

Rae's first instinct was to screw the
letter up in a ball and hurl it into the
bushes. He said he wanted to apologise,
but what did he want to apologise for?
Was it for trying to pin her down with
his arms in such a way that it reminded
her of Andrew? Or was it because he'd
shown his true feelings when she'd told
him Andrew had kissed her, his expression
revealing a mixture of revulsion,
disappointment and self-righteousness?
Whatever it was, she didn't want to
know. It would simply bring back the
memories of her last meeting with
Jamie, and worse, it would once again
remind her of the night she'd been with
Andrew — something she was trying
hard to forget.

How dare he? she thought as she

cycled down the drive towards Mrs Richardson's house. She would tear it up when she got there and put it on the compost heap.

* * *

Mrs Richardson's house was in the middle of what was known as Dunton Plotlands. Years before, farmers had sold off parcels of their land to individuals who over the years had built an enormous variety of homes, ranging from structures that were hardly more than large wooden sheds to smarter brick-built single-storey homes. While houses were being constructed, owners and their families lived in tents, shacks, and in one instance an old railway carriage.

The plots of land had been sold by agents primarily to Londoners, particularly to those in the East End of London where packed tenement blocks jostled for space with factories and sweatshops, and the dire poverty, unemployment and hunger drove some to crime and many to despair. Those who could afford the reasonably cheap prices for a parcel of land in the wilds of the Essex countryside leapt at the chance, and each Friday evening saw an exodus from Fenchurch Street Station as families travelled to Laindon Station with a vast array of tools and other items they needed to turn their Plotland shacks and hovels into homes.

Rae knew that Joanna had been one of those who'd left the East End to find a new life in the Dunton Plotlands and that she'd met Ben, the son of a wealthy landowner, and fallen in love. Ben's mother had been horrified her only son wanted to marry a girl from the East End and had threatened to disinherit Ben, but he'd simply married Joanna anyway and the couple had built a house in Plotlands.

Once his father died, Mrs Richardson realised she couldn't manage the estate on her own and had invited Ben and Joanna to live with her in Priory Hall, but she'd taken every opportunity to make Joanna's life a misery, and finally Ben had decided they would go back to the house they'd built in the Plotlands.

In an unexpected move, Mrs Richardson had insisted Ben and Joanna stay in Priory Hall and suggested she move out. The plan had been that as soon as she found a suitable house, she would buy it, and in the meantime she'd live in Ben and Joanna's house. Inexplicably, Mrs Richardson had remained there, although she insisted on some enlargement to the building and on having a cook and maid — which impressed her neighbours, who secretly called her 'Lady Richardson'.

'Yes?' the young maid said when she opened the door and found a dishevelled Rae on the doorstep.

'I've come to tidy up the garden,' Rae said.

'Good luck. You're going to need it!'

'Who is it, Tilly?' a voice called from inside the house.

'It's a boy come to do the garden, ma'am.'

'I'm a girl!' said Rae crossly, although looking down at the overalls, she could see why the maid had been mistaken. She'd jammed a cap on her head before she'd knocked at the door, knowing that cycling through the lanes had blown her hair into disarray and not wanting to appear too scruffy. In an attempt to forget Jamie and his invitation, she'd pedalled furiously, swerving on some gravel at one point and almost falling off.

'Show him around the back please, Tilly. And keep an eye on him. I shall hold you responsible if anything goes missing.'

'Yes, ma'am,' Tilly called over her shoulder.

'Don't worry, I'll let her know I was mistaken about you being a boy,' Tilly said to Rae as she led her to the back garden and showed her the tool shed.

'What d'you think she'd like me to do first?' Rae asked.

Tilly shrugged. 'Beats me,' she said, 'but trust me, if you do something she

161

don't like, she'll let you know. She's got eyes in the back of her head. She'll be watching us now from the window.'

Tilly had been correct. As soon as Rae dug her spade into the hard clay soil, there was a rapping on the window. Shortly after, it opened and Mrs Richardson leaned out and called, 'You can start over there.' She pointed to the other side of the garden, where brambles had started to creep in from next door's overgrown garden.

Tilly came out an hour later with a glass of water and a biscuit on a plate. 'What d'you say your name was?' she asked. 'Only, Mrs Richardson wants to know.'

'Rae.'

Tilly eyed her doubtfully. 'You sure you're not a boy?'

'No, my real name's Hannah-Rae. My parents were going to call me Hannah if I was a girl and Raymond if I was a boy, after my papa's parents. But in the end, they decided to put the names together.'

Before Rae had finished clearing the brambles, Mrs Richardson emerged from the house, and tapping determinedly with her walking stick, she marched down the path. From her reputation, Rae had imagined she would be a large woman, so this small frail-looking figure took her by surprise.

'You must be the gardener Tilly is having difficulties with!' she said in anything but a small, frail voice.

'Difficulties?' said Rae.

'First, she tells me you're a boy and then she changes her mind, although . . .' Mrs Richardson peered at Rae over the top of her glasses. 'I can quite see her problem. I've never seen a girl attired in overalls before. And then she tells me you have two names, one a boy's and one a girl's. So perhaps you'd be good enough to tell me your real name before I assume you're up to no good.'

Before Rae could answer, Mrs Richardson added, 'But then you are related to my daughter-in-law, so it's only to be expected, I suppose.'

Realising Joanna and their family were being judged on the basis of Rae's appearance and by whatever response she made next, she swallowed and composed herself.

'Good afternoon, Mrs Richardson. Firstly, please may I introduce myself. I am Hannah-Rae Kingsley, and I assure you I am a girl. I expect the confusion has arisen because of my overalls, but I find they are much more practical than skirts, which tend to get tangled in brambles.' She paused, hoping that she hadn't overdone the politeness. It had been as much as she could bring herself to muster. If it hadn't been for Joanna, she'd have flung her fork down and stormed out of the garden, never to return.

But it seemed to have done the trick.

'I see, Hannah-Rae. Well, thank you for clearing that up. I suppose you being a girl explains why you haven't yet managed to clear that patch of brambles. If you don't do it today, I hope you'll be back bright and early tomorrow to finish the job.'

Exactly how Rae managed to say, 'Of course, Mrs Richardson,' she didn't know, but she was not going to be beaten by this rude woman and risk making things worse for Joanna.

'And I hope you've dug up all the roots. I don't want them growing back. They shouldn't be growing there at all . . . ' She glared in the direction of her neighbour's house. ' . . . but Miss Quinn seems incapable of containing her own garden. What a deplorable muddle! Now, when you've finished, don't forget to clean the tools before putting them away.' Mrs Richardson turned and tapped her way back up the path to the house.

Shortly after, Tilly appeared with a slice of cake and glass of milk. 'If you don't mind,' she said apologetically, 'please can you take this over there where she can't see you from the window?' She pointed towards an enormous oak tree. 'It's just that she told me to bring out water and a couple of biscuits, but you've been working so hard, I thought you might like something a bit nicer. Oh, and well done for keeping calm. Mrs Richardson can be a bit, well, critical. Her son's sent over three other gardeners so far and none of them have lasted as long as you! D'you plan to come back tomorrow?'

'Yes,' said Rae, 'I certainly do. I'm not going to give her the satisfaction of making me quit!'

As she put her gardening gloves back in the bicycle basket that evening after tidying away the tools, she saw Jamie's letter and remembered she was going to put it on the compost heap. Well, it was too late now; she wasn't going back to the bottom of the garden just to get rid of it. She took it out of the envelope and looked at it. The writing didn't flow; in fact, the letters were stiff and formal, as though each one had been painstakingly inscribed. She remembered how embarrassed he'd been when he'd told her he was ashamed of his writing and wondered how long it'd taken him to write that single page.

She felt a stab of guilt that she had no intention of meeting him outside Baxter's Tea Rooms the following day. But then, she hadn't asked him to write, nor to come to Laindon. She screwed the letter up into a small ball and threw it back in the basket.

On Wednesday morning, she arrived at Mrs Richardson's early and quietly got the tools she would need out of the garden shed. It promised to be a hot day and she wanted to get the heavy digging out of the way early. And for Joanna's sake, she wanted to make a good impression on Mrs Richardson.

At mid-morning, Rae heard the tap, tap, tap of the old lady's walking stick as she came down the path.

'Good morning, Mrs Richardson,' she said brightly.

'Good morning Hannah-Rae. I see you've already made a start. Splendid, splendid.'

Rae braced herself for criticism, but it appeared there was none. She carried on digging and pulling out roots as if she was not being observed.

'You really are a strange young woman,' Mrs Richardson said finally. 'Are you sure you're related to my daughter-in-law?'

'Yes, Mama and Joanna are cousins.'

'I see. And where do your parents live?'

'Barlstead. It's a little village in Sussex.'

'And does your father work in the village?'

Rae hid a smile. Mrs Richardson had obviously made assumptions about her family based on the fact that she was working in the garden and they were related to Joanna.

'My father is a top physician at the London Hospital in Whitechapel,' Rae said nonchalantly, 'and my mama is training to be a doctor too.'

'Oh!'

No, Mrs Richardson definitely hadn't expected that!

'I was treated in the London Hospital

a few years ago after I fell off a horse. Excellent medical care! First class! And your mama is training to be a doctor too?' Mrs Richardson said.

'Yes.'

'Well, I don't hold with such nonsense myself. Women should be at home, but the world is changing. Perhaps I ought to revise my thinking.' She paused and then added, 'And are you going to follow your parents into medicine, Hannah-Rae?'

'No, I don't think so. I like to be outdoors. But I don't know what I want to do.'

'Well, if you take my advice, you won't spend longer than you need in my daughter-in-law's company. She was a mere typist when she met and ensnared my son. She's nothing more than a scheming minx. I feel you can do better than that.'

'I think that's very unfair to Joanna,' Rae said, feeling anger bubble up inside.

'Nonsense, Hannah-Rae! You need to

take more notice of your elders and betters. Now, I think you'd better carry on. You've missed a bit of root there. I can see it poking up. And make sure you clean the tools and put them away when you've finished.' She turned and walked back up the path.

Later, Tilly came out with cake and milk, and Rae ate and drank under the giant oak tree.

'Well, I see you're still here,' Tilly said. 'Cook bet you'd be gone by midday.'

'I'm not going to let her beat me,' said Rae. 'But how do you and Cook put up with her?'

'Her son pays us double the usual rate to stay. I'm getting married in September and I'm making as much as I can now. But it's hard. She's such a bad-tempered old biddy. Dunton's such a friendly place — all the neighbours help each other out, and there's a real community spirit, but she upsets everyone and no one can stand her. Nobody visits except her son, and he can't wait to get away. It's a shame. But if she can't control her temper and sharp tongue, she's going to have to put up with the loneliness.'

'Tilly! Tilly! Where are you, you dratted girl?' It was Mrs Richardson, calling from the back door.

'No peace for the wicked,' said Tilly, turning to run back to the house.

The brook at the bottom of the garden ensured the soil was damp and heavy to dig, and by the time the sun was overhead, sweat trickled down Rae's back and face. She stopped and mopped her forehead with her sleeve. Tilly's words replayed over and over: *She's such a bad-tempered old biddy and she's going to have to put up with the loneliness*. It reminded her of Pop's description of her own grandmother, who lived in an East End street of friendly neighbours, none of whom wanted anything to do with her. Even her husband and children had deserted her. How sad.

Mama showed signs of becoming like her own mother. Rae tried to remember the last time her mama had cuddled her or spent any real time with her. There were plenty of memories of arguments, the last one being when she'd been sent home from school in disgrace. That, Rae acknowledged, had been her fault, but nevertheless, she had a feeling that Joanna would have handled it with more understanding and kindness.

So what was it that had turned Mama, Gran and Mrs Richardson into such angry, critical women? Perhaps, Rae thought, it ran in families.

And you, Rae, a tiny voice inside her head asked, *are you going to turn into such a woman?*

Of course not! She was nothing like her mama! Yes, from time to time she lost her temper, but as she got older, she knew she'd grow out of it.

But the nagging voice of doubt asked if perhaps she might be growing *into* it.

I've kept my temper with Mrs Richardson, and she's really trying, she told the voice.

Because it suits you, the voice said.

Well, that was true. But she hadn't lost her temper recently, apart from when she received Jamie's letter.

Exactly, said the voice. *He made the effort to contact you so he could apologise and you won't even see him.*

It was true. Rae felt ashamed. She could have at least met him and listened to his apology. But instead, he was now waiting for her outside Baxter's Tea Rooms. She checked her watch. It was twenty-five past two. She wondered if he was still there, but knowing Jamie, he would be.

She piled the tools under the tree out of sight of Mrs Richardson and closed the tool shed door. Later on she'd come back and clean them, but now she had to get to Laindon. The avenues of Plotlands were unmade and rutted, and it was impossible to cycle over them. She wheeled her bicycle over the furrows and grassy tussocks until she reached the smoother streets nearer the High Road, then she mounted and pedalled as fast as she could.

When she arrived at the tea rooms, it was ten past three and there was no sign of him. She peered in through the windows, but he wasn't there, and she got back on her bike and set off for the railway station. A train pulled away from the platform with a hiss of steam, slowly gathering speed.

He'd gone.

But with relief, she realised the train was heading towards London, not Southend where Jamie would be going.

'Oi! Watch what you're doing!' a man shouted at her as she dropped the bicycle on the pavement outside the station and rushed into the ticket office.

Would they let her through on to the platform without a ticket?

'Rae?'

It was Jamie. He was looking at the timetable on the wall when she ran in.

She suddenly caught sight of herself in the reflection of the ticket office window and saw what a fright she looked in her dirty overalls, sweat-streaked face and unkempt hair.

174

'Oh, it's so good to see you!' he said. 'I thought you weren't going to come.' His face lit up with a smile, despite her dishevelled appearance.

'I can't stay long,' she said. 'I've got to get back to work, but I didn't want you to think I hadn't bothered to come.'

'Have you got time for a cup of tea?'

'I'm not going into Baxter's like this,' Rae said, looking down at the mud that was caked over her overalls and boots.

She noted that Jamie had taken a great deal of care with his appearance. He looked so smart and handsome.

'Perhaps I can walk you back to work?' he asked. 'I don't want you to get into trouble.'

She nodded and led him outside to where she'd abandoned her bicycle.

As they walked down the High Road, he told her about his dad's brother, Uncle Gordon, who'd fallen and hurt his back a few weeks before. Since Jamie's father had Alex and lots of men working for him, Jamie had offered to

175

help out in his uncle's boatyard in Leigh-on-Sea.

Rae was amazed at how confident he seemed and how much he'd grown. He was now almost six inches taller than her and his arms were no longer like pipe cleaners. He'd taken his jacket off and she could see his muscles bulging beneath the rolled-up sleeves of his shirt.

It wasn't until they turned off the main road and started down the rutted, bumpy track at the start of Plotlands that he mentioned why he'd wanted to see her.

'I suppose I might as well get it over,' he said without looking at her. 'When I last saw you, I upset you. I'd like to explain and put things right . . . if you'll let me.'

His earlier confidence had gone and he glanced at her quickly to see if she'd allow him to continue. Rae nodded.

'That time you came with your friend Bobby, I overheard her say I was childish —'

'Oh, Jamie, I'm so sorry. I didn't realise you'd heard. And I'm also sorry I didn't put Bobby in her place.'

'No need to apologise. She was right.' He paused. 'But I wasn't sure what to do about it, so I listened to the lads in Dad's yard and I picked up all sorts of things about how a man's supposed to act. They were talking all sorts of nonsense, as it turns out. But I didn't know that then. And when you told me about that . . . that boy, I thought what you needed was for me to . . . well . . . hold you . . . like a man. But I got it all wrong.' His cheeks were now scarlet, and Rae grabbed his arm and stopped him.

'Jamie! I had no idea what was going on in your head. I'm so sorry. I was embarrassed by what I'd done and I thought you found me revolting after I told you Andrew had kissed me . . . and I couldn't bear it.'

'Rae, I could never find you revolting! I was shocked at what you told me, and if I'm honest, I was jealous — but never, ever revolted.'

Jealous? It hadn't crossed her mind he might be jealous. How strange! The whole incident had been nauseating. What was there to be jealous of?

'So, do you forgive me?' he asked.

'There's nothing to forgive.'

She expected him to grin at her and punch her arm jokingly, or perhaps grab her around the waist and swing her round as he would have done before Bobby had disrupted things. She'd have squealed as they spun, and he'd have pretended to become dizzy and stumble, and she'd have insisted he put her down, and then when he did, she'd have punched him playfully and then run away, knowing he'd chase her; and when he caught her, they'd collapse in a heap, laughing until their sides hurt.

But now, he merely smiled and nodded politely, his hands clasped behind his back.

'So,' she said brightly, feeling the need to fill the silence, 'I'd better get back to work. Mrs Richardson'll be after me if I don't clean her tools and tidy away.'

'Yes, of course.'

'Her house is just up there.' Rae pointed further up the avenue.

He nodded, and disappointment washed over her as she realised he was going to leave her. Perhaps she'd never see him again. He'd changed from the fun-loving boy whose company she'd enjoyed to a polite stranger — and she suspected that Bobby's criticism and her silent agreement might have had something to do with it.

'Will you be able to find your way back to the station?' she asked, hoping he'd say no and that he'd wait for her. But she knew he had a good sense of direction; he'd be able to find Laindon Station if he was blindfolded.

He nodded. 'Well goodbye, and thank you for meeting me.' His words were so formal that for a second, she wondered if he was going to put out his hand and shake hers.

She watched him go and hoped he'd turn around, grin and run back, saying 'Fooled you! Of course I'm not leaving you here.' But he kept walking.

With a sigh, she carried on to Mrs Richardson's garden. It occurred to her that if she cleared away quickly, she might catch Jamie up. And she also might escape without encountering Mrs Richardson.

But the old lady had seen her return and was waiting for her by the tree where she'd hidden the tools.

'I thought I made it clear the tools were to be cleaned and stored in the shed.'

'Yes, Mrs Richardson, I'm going to do that now.'

'Well, see that you do! I shall expect you bright and early tomorrow. You don't seem to have progressed much at all today.'

'Yes, Mrs Richardson.'

Rae hurriedly drew some water from the well and cleaned the tools, then dried them and placed them in the shed. When she finished tomorrow, she'd sharpen and oil them, but there was no time now.

There would be no chance she'd catch Jamie before he left, but just to satisfy herself, she'd ride to the station. Perhaps he'd stopped to have tea in Baxter's before he caught the train. It was possible although highly unlikely.

She arrived at the ticket office as a Southend-bound train pulled in and stopped with a hiss of steam and a shudder. Doors opened and slammed and as Rae rushed to the barrier, passengers who'd just arrived pushing past her. But ahead on the platform, just boarding the train, was Jamie.

'Ticket?' said the collector, barring the way with his arm. 'Sorry, miss; you can't proceed without a ticket.'

'Please, I just need to talk to someone. Please!'

Doors slammed, the whistle blew, clouds of steam escaped with a hiss, and the train jerked forward.

Jamie spotted her and lowered the

window, looking at her questioningly.

'Meet me again?' she called but the noise of the train creeping forward drowned her words, and he cupped his hand to his ear to show he hadn't heard.

'Meet her here tomorrow at two o'clock,' the ticket collector bellowed.

Jamie nodded and waved, then was obscured by a cloud of steam as the train picked up speed.

Rae looked at the ticket collector in disbelief. 'Why did you do that? How dare you? You don't know if I'm free tomorrow at two!'

'Look, miss, that poor lad's been here for some time. I thought it strange he let two trains go without getting on, and then I saw his face light up when he saw you and I knew what was what. Turn up or don't turn up, it's no skin off my nose. But it'll be on your conscience if you break his heart.'

'You don't know what you're talking about,' Rae said crossly.

The ticket collector tapped the side of his nose. 'You get to see all sorts of things in this job, miss. Trust me, I knows what's what.'

★   ★   ★

Jamie looked out of the carriage window at the blur of Essex countryside with unseeing eyes. Before him danced the image of Rae; a streak of mud across her forehead, her hair tangled, but still so beautiful. He'd longed to cup her face in his hands and to tell her how much he'd missed her. How she filled his thoughts.

But he hadn't. He'd acted with self-control. He'd remained distant, just as he knew she want. He'd acted like a man.

And it had hurt.

But if that was the only way he could spend time with her, then it would have to be enough. Her voice still rang in his ears — *I met a boy. And he kissed me and it was horrible. And I never want to kiss anyone ever again. Ever!*

That had been very clear.

183

He clenched his fists at the thought of that boy — Andrew, Rae had said his name was.

And yet, Rae had obviously followed him to Laindon station and had wanted to see him again.

He tried to crush the tiny glimmer of hope that now flickered in his heart.

★ ★ ★

Rae got up at first light the next morning. If she started early in the garden, she would feel justified in leaving promptly — and after all, what could Mrs Richardson do? She could ask her not to come back, but even she must realise that there would be a delay while Ben found someone else to clear the garden, during which time the weeds and brambles would once again take hold.

'You're up early, darling,' Joanna said when she found Rae already dressed in her overalls in the kitchen drinking tea on her own.

184

'I wanted to meet a friend this afternoon, so I thought I'd make an early start, if that's all right with you.'

'Of course it is. I can't tell you how grateful Ben and I are that you've taken it on. But I hope my mother-in-law isn't taking advantage of you, Rae. Please don't accept any nonsense.' Joanna sat opposite Rae and sipped her tea. 'Although I think you're capable of giving as good as you get! We come from a family of strong women!'

It was meant as a compliment, Rae knew, but it still made her feel uncomfortable.

'You mean Pop's wife and my mother?'

'Well, yes, and if there are two, there are probably others.'

'But you're not like that, Joanna. You're kind and gentle. Nothing like my mother.'

'Not always, darling. I have my moments. And as for being like your mother, well, we both had very different childhoods. Your mama is driven to achieve things. I have all I want here.'

'Am I going to turn out like Mama and Grandma Ivy?'

'Since you've thought about it enough to ask the question, I'd say that you won't.'

'I'll try not to.'

'But there's a difference between being strong and being bad-tempered, Rae. The problem is deciding where the dividing line lies . . . Anyway, don't let me keep you, if you plan to meet a friend. I didn't know you'd made any friends here.'

'Oh, no, it's someone I've known for a while.' Rae took her cup and saucer to the sink and washed them up.

'Who is it, in case your mama telephones and wants to know?'

'Jamie MacKenzie.' Rae held her breath, waiting for Joanna to query her further, but she merely stood up and with her head cocked on one side said, 'Can you hear Mark? He's teething at the moment. I've been up and down all night.'

The unmistakable wails of a baby could just be heard, and Joanna turned to go to him.

'Well, have fun today with your friend and don't work too hard this morning.'

That wouldn't have happened if Rae had been at home. Mama used to complain she spent too much time with Jamie. Although on reflection, it probably wasn't because he was a boy, but simply because he was from a different class — a lower class. It seemed that Grandma Ivy and Mama were both snobs. Was she a snob? Absolutely not! That was one difference between her and her mother and grandmother. So it wasn't inevitable that she follow them.

She could be her own person.

When Rae reached the gate, Tilly opened the front door and put her finger to her lips, then walked down the path to meet her.

'There's good news and there's bad news this morning,' Tilly said quietly, looking back at the house, over her shoulder. 'Although the bad news is bad for me and the good news is good for you.'

'What's happened?'

'Mrs Richardson has one of her headaches, so I'm going to be in strife all day. That's the bad news.'

'And the good news?'

'You've got the day off. She doesn't want you in the garden — as she put it, 'making all that racket'. But apparently she wants you back tomorrow. I pointed out it was Saturday tomorrow but she bit my head right off.'

'Shall I sharpen the tools or do something quiet?' Rae asked, feeling guilty.

'No, I wouldn't risk upsetting her.'

'Then I'll just pick some flowers before I go.'

Rae crept around the garden, snipping off rosebuds from the overgrown bushes and finding blooms from plants which were being overtaken by weeds. As soon as she had the brambles under control, she'd start pruning the plants that were supposed to be there. Ben had plenty of gardening books in the library and she'd been reading up about garden care.

Rae caught Cook's eye through the kitchen window and passed her the bunch of flowers, then with a wave, she picked up her bicycle and started for home. She'd deliberately avoided thinking about how she was going to satisfy Mrs Richardson and then get home in time to wash and change before meeting Jamie at the station at two. If necessary, she'd have worked until the last minute and then arrived at the station in the same state as yesterday — dirty and sweaty, in muddy overalls and boots.

Now she didn't have to worry.

No one was home when she arrived back at Priory Hall, and after a wash, she wondered what to wear. It was another beautiful day with clear blue skies, and she looked forlornly in her wardrobe. Most of the clothes she'd worn the previous summer no longer fitted, but as she'd worn either warm clothes or her school uniform since then, Mama hadn't bought her anything new. Of course, if she'd finished the summer term and gone home under normal conditions, her mother would have taken her out to buy her different clothes. While she'd been at Joanna's she'd either worn overalls or a blouse and skirt, which although slightly small and rather dowdy, were still all right. She had one dress which the previous year had been her favourite, but it made her look so young, with the bow at its Peter Pan collar, the short puff sleeves and the full body with a matching belt, that she hadn't planned on wearing it again. But now she would have to. It was slightly too short but at least it wasn't as tight as the blouse across her chest.

Rae stared at her reflection in the mirror and cringed. She looked like an adult actress she'd once seen who was playing the part of a little girl. But it would have to do. It was either the dress or the overalls. And if she didn't hurry up, she risked being late again, despite having all morning to herself to get ready.

It was twenty to two when Rae arrived at the station. She looked out for the ticket collector so she could avoid him, but he was obviously not on duty, and she studied the posters on the walls advertising Southend-on-Sea and Westcliff-on-Sea while she waited in the ticket office for the next train from their direction.

Five minutes later, a train pulled in with squeal of brakes and hiss of steam and then doors opened and people began to pass through the ticket barrier. She scanned the faces, not expecting Jamie to be on the early train, but he was there behind a large woman who was carrying two hatboxes and blocking the way. He smiled and waved at Rae, and she saw with dismay how handsome he looked in his suit, wondering what he must be thinking of her in such a childish dress.

'Well,' Jamie said when the large

woman with the hatboxes finally found her ticket and moved out of the way, 'that was a surprise yesterday. I didn't expect to see you again. What did you have in mind?'

'What did I have in mind?' she asked.

'Well, yes, when you asked me to meet you today at two. Was there a reason?'

Before she'd thought it through, she said, 'Oh, no, that was the ticket collector.'

Jamie looked puzzled.

'I called out to ask you if we could meet again but you didn't hear, so he took it upon himself to ask you to come today.'

The smile slipped from Jamie's face. 'Oh, I see. I'm so sorry, Rae, I had no idea. Well, there'll be a train along shortly, I'll just go home.'

She couldn't bear to see the disappointment on his face. How could she have been so silly? Why hadn't she pretended it'd been her idea? She could've said she wondered if they could go to Baxter's for tea, but instead she'd been honest and hurt him. 'Oh no! Jamie, I did want to see you — '

'But just not today,' he said dejectedly.

'No, I did! Really! It's just that the ticket inspector got in before me.' Even to Rae's ears, that explanation sounded ridiculous. And then, without thinking, she said, 'I wonder if we might go to Southend. I've been looking at the posters and it looks so nice . . . that is, if you don't mind?'

'Yes, you'll love it! There're loads of boats to look at. And there's the pier, of course.'

Somehow she'd managed to rescue the situation, as he now seemed full of enthusiasm — just like she remembered him.

When the train arrived at the station at Southend, Rae was surprised to see so many people. It reminded her of the times she'd been to London with Papa, although here the pace was more leisurely, presumably because so many people were on holiday. Jamie stepped forward into the swirl of holidaymakers and she almost lost sight of him before he offered her his arm. She tucked her hand beneath it with relief and held on tightly as they made their way to the Esplanade. It hadn't been so long ago that she'd grabbed his arm as she pulled him under the surface while they were splashing in the water at Cranston's Point. Now she couldn't encircle his biceps with her hand. He felt so strong, steering her along through the crowds, and when they arrived at the water's edge, she was disappointed when he released her hand.

They walked along the Esplanade, admiring the boats and remembering times they'd spent on the *Wild Spirit*; and when they reached what Jamie told her was the longest pier in the world, he bought tickets for the tiny electric train that ran from the shore, travelling about a mile to the pier head.

Once back on the Esplanade, Jamie bought them both ice creams, which they ate on the beach while they watched the tide recede, leaving small boats lying on their sides, stranded on the mud.

Rae took notice of the dresses and outfits worn by the women who walked with their arms tucked into their husband's or sweetheart's arms. Summery dresses and elegant hats, even parasols to match. She couldn't bear to look down at her little girl's dress. No wonder Jamie kept his distance from her. He was treating her like a younger sister. And that, she knew, was what they looked like — dutiful brother taking his younger sister on an outing.

'Shall we go on the rollercoaster?' Jamie asked as they wandered through the Kursaal amusement park, looking at all the fairground attractions. The ticket seller for the Caterpillar Ride must have noticed their indecision, and called out, 'Roll up, roll up! Come on, Sir! Take yer sweetheart on the Caterpillar! You'll never 'ave a better excuse for a cuddle, if yer know what I mean!' He winked at

Jamie, who blushed and veered away from the ride.

Rae's stomach sank. Jamie was embarrassed because of her. How humiliating!

'I think, if you don't mind, Jamie, I'd like to go home. I'm suddenly rather tired.'

He nodded. 'Yes, of course.' He turned and pointed in the opposite direction. 'The station's this way.'

Their progress was slow through the throng of families and couples who strolled and chattered excitedly, soaking up the holiday atmosphere.

They finally arrived at the station, and Rae got out her return ticket so she could disappear as quickly as possible through the barrier and make her way home. The sooner she was gone, the sooner Jamie would be rid of her, but when she turned to thank him, he'd gone.

She told herself she was relieved that her embarrassment was now over and that she would soon be home, but deep down she was disappointed that Jamie had been so keen to get rid of her. He hadn't even said goodbye; just delivered her to the station and then left.

She sat down on a bench on the platform and closed her eyes, holding back the tears.

'Rae?'

When she looked up, Jamie was standing in front of her with a concerned expression on his face. 'What are you doing?'

'Going home, of course. What are you doing?'

'Coming with you,' he said. 'I had to buy a ticket and when I looked around, you'd gone. What's the matter?'

She stared at him in amazement. Of course he knew what the matter was! Surely he didn't want her to actually say the words *You are embarrassed by me and I'm so ashamed, I'm going home*, did he?

'Nothing,' she said. 'I just want to go home.'

'Well, you'd better come with me then,' he said with a smile.

How dare he laugh at her?

'Why don't you just leave me alone? I'm quite capable of finding my own way home!' she said.

He sighed. 'I would leave you alone but I'm not sure you *are* capable of finding your own way home. This is the wrong platform. If you get on the next train, you'll end up in Shoeburyness.'

Rae sighed. Her humiliation was complete.

'Come on,' Jamie said, 'let's cross to the other platform or we'll miss the next train. Now I've bought my ticket, I might as well take you as far as Laindon, and then if you prefer, I'll leave you there. I can see you've had enough of me.'

He walked off towards the footbridge. She caught him as he was halfway up the stairs. 'What d'you mean you can see I've had enough of you? I didn't say that! Surely it's the other way around?'

'Come on,' he said, grabbing her hand. 'There's a train coming, quick!'

They arrived on the correct platform out of breath, and Jamie held the door open for Rae, then climbing into the carriage after her, he slammed the door. The day-trippers were obviously still enjoying the delights of Southend, and so Jamie and Rae were the only passengers to board the London-bound train. The guard blew a piercing blast on his whistle and waved his flag as a puff of steam blew and the train lurched forward with a chug, chug of the pistons.

Jamie sat opposite Rae and leaned forward, his elbows on his knees. 'I've obviously upset you — again. And I tried so hard not to. But since we're stuck on this train until Laindon, perhaps you'd be good enough to tell me what I've done. Unless you want to get off at an earlier station and wait for another train, of course!'

'But you haven't upset me!' she said in amazement. 'It's me who's upset you!'

They stared at each other in bewilderment.

'Perhaps you'd care to explain?' he asked with a puzzled frown. If she hadn't seen the hurt in his eyes, she'd have insisted that he explain, but she had to acknowledge he'd paid for her train fares, ice creams and everything else that afternoon, so perhaps *she* owed *him* an explanation. And if she hurried up and got it over before they arrived at Leigh-on-Sea, he could get out and leave her to carry on the journey home on her own.

'I . . . I could see how uncomfortable you were when that man on the Caterpillar Ride assumed we were sweethearts and . . . well, I couldn't blame you. So I thought if I went home, it might save you more embarrassment.'

'Well,' said Jamie, 'I *was* embarrassed, it's true. I'd tried so hard to make it look like we were just friends, and I knew if anyone thought otherwise, it'd upset you.'

The train pulled into Chalkwell Station. The next stop would be Leigh-on-Sea. Rae and Jamie continued to stare at each other.

'This isn't making any sense,' Rae said. Jamie obviously needed things spelling out in more detail. 'That man didn't upset me. It wouldn't have bothered me if he'd thought we were sweethearts. In fact, I'd have been quite proud, but — '

'Proud he assumed we were together?' Jamie was amazed. 'But I thought I acted too young for you. I was trying hard to be grown up — '

'So was I! But it's really difficult when you look like this!' she said, looking down at the dress and pulling the skirt angrily.

'Rae! You look fine. It doesn't matter what you wear, you always look beautiful to me.'

She stared at him with an expression of incredulity, 'But this dress is . . . hideous.'

'You wore it last year. And it looked lovely then — '

'Exactly! I wore it last year!'

'But?'

'It's a little girl's dress. This year it doesn't even fit. There were so many ladies at Southend out with their men, and I felt ashamed that you had to put up with me.'

'Rae! I wasn't putting up with anything. I loved having you with me.'

'Then why did you make sure you were always several inches away from me? You offered me your arm and then as soon as we got to the Esplanade, you almost pushed me away!'

'That's a slight exaggeration; I did nothing of the sort. I simply thought you wouldn't want people to think you were with me other than as a friend.'

The train pulled into Leigh-on-Sea station.

'Aren't you getting out?' Rae asked.

'Of course not! I'm taking you to Laindon. And anyway, I still don't really understand what's going on! You seem to think I'm embarrassed to be seen with you and that's simply not true. I was keeping my distance so I didn't embarrass *you*. There's nothing I'd have liked more than to have walked along arm in arm with you.' He stood up, and then sitting down next to her, he took her hand. 'The first time I set eyes on you, I fell for you, Rae. I know people would scoff and say I was too young, and perhaps they're right, but I know how I felt. You took my breath away.'

'Not that day I punched you?' Rae asked aghast.

Jamie smiled at her. 'You were the most beautiful thing I'd ever seen. You still are!'

'Oh, Jamie, I'm so sorry. I thought you were staring because you found me ridiculous in that dreadful coat my mother made me wear! I had no idea you felt like that!'

'Your free spirit is all part of what I . . . ' He hesitated. ' . . . like about you.'

It had sounded like he was about to say *what I love about you.*

This was all such a shock. She'd had no idea he felt like that, despite Bobby telling her Jamie had puppy eyes for her. Rae had simply told her to shut up.

'I know you don't feel the same, Rae,' he said sadly.

'No, it's not that! I don't know how I

feel. Bobby and I used to go to the cinema each Saturday afternoon, and we watched all sorts of Hollywood films and after a while, I started to believe that's what life would be like when I grew up. I don't know why it didn't occur to me that it's not like my parents or anyone else I know. And then when I went with Bobby to meet that boy, things were so different. So grimy. I wasn't sure what to believe, so I blocked it from my mind. But I do like you, Jamie. I've always enjoyed being with you.'

He looked disappointed but resigned.

'Yesterday, when I realised I might not see you again, I couldn't bear it,' she said, 'But I'm not sure how I feel. It's all so confusing. Can you wait until I've sorted things out in my mind?'

He smiled then. 'I'll wait for you forever, Rae. But don't worry, I won't pressure you for anything — not spending time with me, or . . . well, anything.'

'D'you mean things like kissing?' Rae

asked and blushed.

Jamie nodded.

'That's good,' said Rae, 'because I'm not sure I'm going to like that part of things.' She carried on, despite his disappointment. Surely it was best now to be completely honest?

'Andrew had blubbery lips and his eyes were cold when he kissed me. It's not something I want to remember . . . or repeat. It was like . . . like . . . well, kissing a haddock,' she said and to her surprise, Jamie laughed.

'I don't think haddocks have blubbery lips!'

'Well, that's what he reminded me of!' Rae said, and joined in the laughter. Suddenly, life seemed so good. They continued to laugh at the thought of Andrew with his puckered-up, blubbery haddock lips until the train pulled into Laindon.

From time to time, despite their aching sides, they still burst into giggles as Jamie walked Rae home to Priory Hall.

That night Rae lay in bed going over the strange events of the day. There was plenty to think about, but the one memory which stayed with her was when Jamie left her at the gate. He'd kissed the tips of his fore and middle finger, then placed them gently against Rae's cheek.

'See you next Saturday,' he said, and then turned and walked away; but unlike the previous day, when he'd left her, he turned back and waved.

5

The following Saturday afternoon, Rae and Jamie met as arranged at Hadleigh Castle. They'd decided to cycle to a point halfway between Leigh-on-Sea and Laindon, but since neither of them were familiar with any of the villages, Jamie suggested they meet near the unmistakable ruin of the castle which stood on a hill overlooking the Thames. It meant a slightly longer ride for Rae than Jamie, but since he often had difficulty getting away from his uncle's boatyard early, it made more sense. It also meant that neither of their families knew about their meetings.

'Not that there's anything wrong with us spending time together,' Jamie said, 'but if my uncle tells Dad, he won't be happy. And I don't know how your cousin Joanna will feel. I expect she'll have to tell your mother.'

Saturday afternoons were spent sitting on the hill in the sunshine, watching the boats and barges sail up and down the Thames, and on the odd occasion when it rained, they explored Hadleigh and Benfleet and found a tea shop where they could shelter.

Ben had asked one of his farm hands to take over the gardening duties at Priory Hall while Joanna was busy with Mark, which allowed Rae to spend more time at Mrs Richardson's taming the garden and bringing it back under control. Miraculously, the old lady seemed to tolerate Rae, and although she was often sharp, she treated Rae well, even paying her for her time.

'I think she recognises your strength of character, Rae,' Joanna said with a smile. 'You're the only person she isn't rude to.'

Uncle Gordon's back was gradually improving and Jamie had more free time, so sometimes if he finished work early, he cycled to Dunton, and when he arrived at Mrs Richardson's, he whistled a tune:

Alive, alive, oh
Alive, alive, oh
Crying 'cockles and mussels, alive,
  alive, oh'

It was from the song 'Molly Molone' and was their pre-arranged signal; Rae would pretend to go to the tool shed for something and wave to let him know she'd heard. He'd carry on to a small lake set in a wooded area not far from the house and wait for her to join him when she'd finished. Then he'd walk her home across the fields.

Although Mrs Richardson's garden was one of the largest on Plotlands, Rae had worked so hard that there wasn't enough to keep her there each day, and she feared she would lose the freedom of coming and going without anyone keeping an eye on her.

Uncle Gordon was also spending more time in his boatyard, and Jamie suspected that as soon as his uncle was back at work full time, there would be no reason to stay on and his father would ask him to return.

And then, of course, September was fast approaching, when Rae would be expected back at school.

'I don't think I can bear it,' Rae said gloomily as they sat in the shade next to the lake.

'Well, I'll probably be back at Dad's by the time you come home for Christmas,' Jamie said, trying to think positively. 'I'll see you then.'

'It won't be the same, though, will it?' Rae said. 'And it's months away.'

The following day when Jamie arrived, Rae was at the bottom of the garden hammering a new fence post into the ground, and she didn't hear the distinctive whistle.

A rustling from the garden next door caught her attention, and she wondered if the badger or whatever had caused the damage to the fence was trapped. But it was a tall, willowy woman parting some of the overgrown vegetation in her garden.

'I'm so sorry to startle you, my dear,

but I thought you might want to know your young gentleman friend is outside whistling his little heart out waiting for you.'

Rae gasped. How did this woman know Jamie was whistling for her?

'It's all right, my dear, your secret's safe with me. Now I suggest you hurry up before he thinks you're not here and goes.'

'Th . . . thank you,' said Rae, putting the hammer down and running towards the avenue.

'I was beginning to think you'd left for the day,' Jamie said when she finally caught up with him further along the avenue.

Rae told him about Miss Quinn, the lady next door.

'D'you think she'll tell Mrs Richardson?' Jamie asked.

'I don't think so. Mrs Richardson's often very rude about her and she doesn't keep her voice down, so I wouldn't be surprised if Miss Quinn heard. Anyway, she said our secret's safe with her.'

'I came to tell you some news. You know Uncle Gordon's going to be back at work full time from next week and we thought I might have to go back home?'

Rae nodded.

'Well, one of my cousins is going to buy into a cockle-fishing business, so he won't be around so much to help Uncle. That means I'll be staying, at least for a while.'

'Once I go back to school, it won't matter if you're here, home or in Scotland,' she said gloomily. 'I won't get to see you much.'

Rae suddenly remembered she'd taken her pullover off earlier and left it at the bottom of the garden.

'I'd better go and get it. Will you wait for me?'

Jamie nodded.

Rae found the pullover draped over the fence and hurried back up the path, but Mrs Richardson intercepted her. 'Where have you been, Hannah-Rae? I looked out earlier to see why you'd stopped that infernal hammering and you weren't there. I pay for you to work, not stand around idling. So where were you?'

Before Rae could answer, a voice came from next door. 'I'm so sorry, Mrs Richardson — I was speaking to your gardener. I take full blame.'

'Well, I . . . that is . . . ' Mrs Richardson blustered.

Before she could regain her composure, Miss Quinn added, 'I would like to speak to Hannah-Rae about the possibility of sorting out my garden. With your permission, of course.'

'Certainly not!' Mrs Richardson said.

'It's just that it would be a shame if all her hard work in your garden was undone by fly-away seeds from all the weeds in my garden. And, as you can see . . . ' She held her hands up. ' . . . I have arthritis, so it's not easy for me to do my own digging now.'

Mrs Richardson looked at the claw-like hands her neighbour was displaying.

'I would pay her well, of course,'

Miss Quinn said, 'but perhaps you'd both like to think it over. I shall be in tomorrow, Hannah-Rae, if you'd care to call, and we can discuss arrangements. Good evening to you both.' She nodded and walked back to her house.

'Well, the nerve of the woman!' said Mrs Richardson. 'Should you accept her offer, I expect my garden to take precedence, Hannah-Rae,' Mrs Richardson said, and tapped her way back to her house.

Rae ran back to where Jamie was waiting for her.

'What is it? What's happened?' he asked. 'You look really happy!'

'I think I have a plan, and it might be a way of staying at Priory Hall if Joanna will allow.'

Rae told him about how Miss Quinn had stepped in to save her having to explain where she'd been when Mrs Richardson had looked for her and about her proposal.

'The only thing is, I'm not sure if she meant it about me working in her garden. Suppose she only said that to throw Mrs Richardson off the scent?'

'I suppose you'll find out tomorrow. But anyway, it looks terribly overgrown. You're not going to be able to get that in order before you go back to school.'

'That's my plan,' said Rae. 'I'm not going back to school. I'm going to work.'

'But won't your parents be disappointed? They might not let you leave.'

'I'll have to find out. But I'm not clever enough to be anything like a doctor, and I don't want to work anywhere indoors. I love it outside.'

That evening as they said goodbye, she expected Jamie to kiss his two fingers as usual and touch her cheek, but instead he brushed her lips with his fingertips, leaving his kiss there and making her shiver with pleasure. She looked down at her muddy hands. She wanted to kiss her fingers and place them on his mouth but they were much too dirty. The next time they met, she would make sure her hands were clean.

And she hoped he would stroke her lips again.

She'd touched his face before, during their horseplay; nose-pulling, pretend slaps, even that shameful punch on the nose; but as she imagined kissing her fingers and placing them on his lips, she shivered with desire, warmth radiating through her.

How strange that on the day she'd decided what she wanted to do with her life, her mind wasn't full of plans for the future; it was reflecting on what Jamie's lips would feel like beneath her fingertips.

*   *   *

The following morning, Rae knocked at Miss Quinn's door. The paint was beginning to peel and the areas around the letterbox and keyhole were scratched and worn. In fact, the entire house seemed tired and shabby.

Rae was nervous. It seemed too good to be true. Why should a woman put herself out for a stranger in the way Miss Quinn had for Rae?

'Call me Ada,' Miss Quinn said as she led Rae into her house. 'I'm not one for standing on ceremony.'

Judging by the unruly garden, Rae expected the house to be untidy too, so she was surprised to fmd it clean and neat. Almost bare, Rae thought without lots of ornaments and photographs in frames or pictures on the walls. It was as if Ada had just moved in and not yet unpacked all the keepsakes that older ladies such as Mrs Richardson seemed to have collected during their lifetimes.

Ada shooed the black and white cat from the sofa and invited Rae to sit while she made tea.

'Titan! Leave Hannah-Rae alone,' she said when she returned and found the cat sitting on Rae's lap.

'Please call me Rae. And I think I took his seat, so I'm quite happy to tickle his ears in return.'

'Well, Rae, you've certainly won him over. He doesn't take to new people, so he must have seen something very special in you. Now, shall we get down to business? You've seen how overgrown the garden is. I'm afraid I suffer with arthritis, so I find it very difficult to use tools. Do you think you'd be able to help me out in the garden? I'd pay well and you could work when it suited you. I wouldn't even mind if you slipped off with your young man from time to time.' Her eyes sparkled as she smiled.

'Oh, he's not really my young man. He's just a friend,' Rae said quickly, her cheeks reddening.

'Not your young man? Well, you'd better hurry up and claim him before some other young lady beats you to it! Are you sure *he* doesn't think he's your young man? He seems to spend a lot of time standing outside whistling for you.'

'Please don't tell Mrs Richardson,' said Rae. 'We really are just friends, but I don't think she'd approve and I've managed to keep it from her so far.'

'Your secret's safe with me,' Ada said

and then added wistfully, 'I'm very good at keeping secrets . . . Now, what do you think of my proposal? Do you think you could tidy up my garden?'

When Rae got home, she told Joanna she didn't want to go back to school in September and asked if she could pay to stay on in Priory Hall.

'I'll get more clients and then I'll be able to pay you a lot,' she said.

'Darling, I think it's wonderful you've got a plan, but are you sure people will employ a female gardener? Some people are so set in their ways.'

'There are quite a few ladies on their own in the district, and Ada said she'd rather not have a strange man around the house. Perhaps others might feel more comfortable with me. I'd like to find out anyway. How d'you think Mama will take the news?'

Joanna winced. 'Hmm, I don't think she's going to be happy. I think it best if I invite her over at the weekend and you can discuss it.'

'It's absolutely out of the question, Hannah-Rae!' Mama said. 'You're going back to St Helena's in September and that's the end to it!'

'Amelia,' Papa said, 'perhaps we ought to discuss it.'

'Discuss it? What's there to discuss? I fought tooth and nail for an opportunity to study. And our daughter wants to abandon hers to dig up weeds! She leaves school over my dead body.'

'But you were stopped from doing what you wanted to do when you were young and you've always resented it. Is it right we stop Rae from doing what she wants to do? Might she one day resent us?' Papa said.

'Resent us? After everything we've done for her!'

There was silence in the drawing room. Ben and Joanna sent each other silent messages with their eyes, Joe looked out of the window, Faye and Jack watched the adults in horrified fascination, Mark began to cry, and Rae glared at her parents.

'I think,' said Papa, 'we ought to perhaps go for a walk. This is the height of rudeness. We've been invited to Joanna and Ben's home, Amelia, and the least we can do is remain civil.'

'Yes, of course,' Mama said. 'I apologise, Joanna. It was a bit of a shock, that's all.'

'Yes, I understand,' Joanna said, picking up Mark and rocking him back to sleep.

Mama and Papa went for a walk in the garden, and through the window Rae watched Mama gesticulating wildly and Papa making placatory motions with his hands.

'Well, you've done it this time, Rae old girl!' said Joe.

It wasn't possible to determine the outcome from her parents' faces as they returned. Papa looked determined. Mama looked angry.

'We think the best thing to do is to wait for a week and let everyone think

221

this over carefully,' said Papa. 'We're hoping Rae may change her mind, but I'm very impressed at how she's beginning to take responsibility for her life.'

Presumably, Mama isn't impressed, thought Rae, but at least her parents hadn't both said no and she had a week to convince them she knew what she was doing and could be trusted. She would do her utmost in that time to find some clients, and then her parents would find it harder to send her back to school.

'And you're sure you're all right with Hannah-Rae staying with you, Joanna?' Mama asked.

'Of course! She's been a marvellous help to me and I know my mother-in-law's extremely pleased with all her work. And the lady next door must be impressed if she's asked Rae to do her garden. Rae's a lovely girl — a credit to you, Amelia. She's become part of the family. And she's made friends here, too. Well, one friend, anyway — haven't you, Rae?'

Rae gulped. Now wasn't the time to bring up Jamie, surely? She nodded, hoping Joanna wasn't going to say anything more.

'And is your friend still at school?' Mama asked.

Rae shook her head.

'So, what does . . . ' Mama paused, waiting for someone to fill in the name.

'Janey,' said Joanna.

'So, what does Janey do for a living?'

* * *

There had been a lot of shouting after that.

There would be no point lying. Rae explained that *his* name was *Jamie*.

Mama had been furious with Rae for spending time with a boy unsupervised. 'I'd have thought you'd have learned a lesson from that dreadful Bobby!' And she'd been angry with Joanna for not keeping an eye on Rae.

'It's not Joanna's fault!' Rae said. 'It was a misunderstanding. I thought she

223

knew I was with Jamie. I didn't know she'd assumed I was with a girl!'

'Who is this Jamie, anyway?' Papa asked.

'Jamie MacKenzie from MacKenzie Boatyard.'

'What's he doing around here?'

'He's helping his uncle in his boatyard in Leigh-on-Sea.'

'It doesn't matter who the boy is, Hannah-Rae, or whether you know him or not. You should still have been honest,' Mama said.

And Joanna remained silent, although Rae knew she felt as though she'd been tricked.

In the end, it was decided that Rae would stay until it was time to go back to school. Mama and Papa were planning to sell their house in Barlstead and buy a place in Chelsea to save the daily journeys on the train, and they were in the middle of packing up their belongings. Papa would return with Rae's school things and then take her directly to St Helena's at the beginning of term. Until then, Rae would be allowed to work at Ada's and Mrs Richardson's but was not allowed to see Jamie.

'But Papa,' Rae said, 'you like Jamie!'

'It's not about liking the boy or not liking him, Rae. It's the fact that you were deceitful.'

There was no point denying it, as neither Mama nor Papa was prepared to listen.

In one afternoon, Rae had lost the fight to leave school, lost Joanna's trust, and lost not one but two homes — she wouldn't have a chance to say goodbye to the house at Barlstead, and in two weeks' time she'd have to leave Priory Hall, a place she'd come to think of as home.

She placed the tiny boat Jamie had given her that first Christmas on her bedside table and cried herself to sleep that night, vowing that as soon as she was old enough, she'd leave with Jamie to travel the world. If she kept on the move, then it wouldn't matter that she didn't belong anywhere.

'I see. Well, it's kind of you to come and tell me, Hannah-Rae,' Mrs Richardson said when she learned that Rae would be returning to school in September. 'I shall be sad to see you go,' she added to Rae's amazement, 'but I agree with your mother and father. School is important and you must do as your parents say. Perhaps when you return to Priory Hall, you'd be good enough to ask my son to arrange for another gardener? Not that much will grow over winter, but I've got used to having it well-kept, and I don't want to see it descend into chaos again. Perhaps when you go and see Miss Quinn, you'd suggest she find a gardener too, so that the work you've done so far on her wilderness will not be undone.'

Tilly and Cook expressed their sadness at Rae leaving, and Cook even baked a fruit cake, although she said it'd been without Mrs Richardson's knowledge and it might be best if Rae ate her slice out of sight under the large oak tree. She also wrapped a large wedge in cloth and gave it to Rae to take home.

Rae had expected Mrs Richardson to be angry about the inconvenience of finding someone else to look after her garden, so she'd been quite touched that the old lady seemed almost sad she wouldn't be back.

But it was Ada who Rae was dreading telling about her return to school. She'd grown fond of the quiet, dignified woman with the sad eyes. Unlike her neighbour who'd never invited Rae into her house, Ada always made tea for them both before Rae started gardening. Titan curled up on Rae's lap while they sat together and talked about France.

Ada had been the only person Rae had confided in about her plans to travel with Jamie when they were both older. The only other people who might have understood were Joanna and Ben, but if they'd known, Rae suspected they

227

would feel obliged to tell Mama. And although her parents wouldn't be able to stop her when she was old enough, she knew there'd be pressure from them to 'behave with more common sense' now.

But Ada had spent long enough working in France to be fluent in the language and to have developed a love for the people and places she'd visited, although she was rather hazy about why she'd gone to France in the first place. She preferred instead to talk about her jobs in different cafés and shops as she travelled from the north to the south.

For a time in Paris, she'd been a life model for an artist who'd begged her to pose for him because, he said, he admired her long legs. She'd spent many hours draped in silk, propped against a wooden post in his freezing attic studio while he magically transformed her on his canvas into a Greek goddess leaning against a marble pillar. He'd never made any money, as far as she knew, and eventually she'd left Paris and travelled south to Nice, and worked as a maid for an American family in a huge villa on the seafront. She'd stayed with the Stamfords until they'd returned to Chicago, and then Ada had decided it was time to return to England.

'Now my travelling days are over,' she said sadly, 'I don't have the energy anymore. But you, Rae, you must follow your heart. There are so many wonderful places to see.'

Rae sighed. It all seemed such a long time in the future. And before then, she had the prospect of school, and that meant not seeing Jamie for months.

'And what will your young man be doing while you're at school?' Ada asked, almost reading Rae's thoughts.

'He'll be here, I suppose, helping his uncle. But I can't bear that I won't be able to see him. It's all so unfair. It's not like I lied about him. It was all a misunderstanding. But even though everyone knows it was a mistake, they still act as though I'd been deceitful, and Mama, particularly, doesn't even like to hear

Jamie's name mentioned.'

'I expect your mama doesn't realise how grown up you are.'

'It's strange,' said Rae, 'that you're the second person who's said that to me. If you and Thérèse can see it, why doesn't Mama?'

'Well, don't underestimate how hard it is to be a mother, Rae. I wish I'd realised that many years ago, then I wouldn't have judged my own mother so harshly. But we lost touch. There were too many bitter words spoken, and after a while there was no taking them back.'

Rae was disappointed. Despite Ada being an adult, she was the only one that Rae knew apart from Thérèse, who didn't uphold the same dull, boring ideas. And now Ada seemed to be making excuses for her mother. It was as if grown-ups always stuck together. Rae wondered what Thérèse would have had to say about it, but she would never see Thérèse again because apparently she'd had a big row with Mama about not being a good mother before she'd left.

'So you're saying I should do everything Mama tells me, like forgetting Jamie?' Rae asked.

To her surprise, Ada said, 'No, not at all. It's hard being a mother and they often make mistakes. They may not mean to, but no one's perfect. It's up to each person to do what's right, regardless of what other people say. Of course, children need guidance until they're old enough to know better; but after having spent time with you, Rae, I feel you've reached that time. Live by your conscience. And as for Jamie, if you feel the way you say you do, then don't let anyone ever persuade you otherwise. *Ever!*' she added with such force, Titan looked up at his mistress, jumped off Rae's lap and squeezed behind the sofa.

'You never know how life's going to turn out,' Ada said. 'You have to grab every chance of happiness, because that moment may be all you have.'

Her voice, usually so calm, was now passionate and her face had become haunted. She stood up and walked to the sideboard, where she opened a drawer and took out an envelope.

'This,' she said, taking a sepia photograph out, 'was Walter, my fiancé. He died in the trenches in northern France during the last war.' She handed the picture to Rae. It had been taken in a French photographic studio and at the top was written, *To my dearest Ada, with love from your own Walter.*

'I'm so sorry, Ada. How dreadful.'

Ada bit her bottom lip and tears gathered in her eyes.

'I know people say I should be over it by now. But the truth is, Rae, I never got over losing Walter. And I never will . . . If there's any chance you can find happiness with your young man, then you need to explore that possibility. You never know how much time you have on this earth. I was the eldest daughter in a large family and each time my father came home from the sea, he added another one. My poor mother was exhausted and she relied on me to care for the other children. So when Walter asked me to marry him, she forbade it. She said he wasn't right for me and made up all sorts of excuses, but the truth was, she couldn't cope without me. I didn't realise that until much later. But if Walter had been a married man, he wouldn't have been conscripted so early on in the war. We might have had some time together before he'd had to join up. But I did as my mother asked and waited . . .'

'Ada, I'm so sorry,' Rae said, not sure what to do. She decided she couldn't simply sit there as if Ada's words had not touched her, so she put her arm around her shoulders.

Finally Ada patted her hand and said, 'You're a good girl, Rae. I know you'll do the right thing. Whatever that turns out to be.'

Later, on her way home, Rae realised why Ada had gone to France — she'd wanted to be near Walter.

In 1939, towards the end of the summer term, Mama and Papa were called into school by the headmistress, Miss Frost.

'I'm afraid, Mr and Mrs Kingsley, that Hannah-Rae has not applied herself to her studies this year. Other than geography and French, her marks have been consistently poor and her attitude is appalling. I gave her a second chance after the Roberta Taylor-Gale incident but her behaviour has been unacceptable. I'm afraid your daughter will not be returning to St Helena's next academic year.'

The drive back to Chelsea passed in silence. Unusually, Mama was too shocked to speak, but the shouting would start soon, Rae thought.

Well, I did tell them I didn't want to go back to school. Nevertheless, it still hurt to be rejected.

The house her parents had bought in Chelsea was a large Victorian building with lofty ceilings and spacious rooms. It was like staying in a hotel, Rae thought. Cold and impersonal. But it had a post box on the corner of the street, and the first thing she did on entering her bedroom was to write to Jamie telling him about her dishonourable exit from school and warning him not to send any letters, either to school because it was unlikely Miss Frost would bother to pass them on, or to the house in Chelsea in case it angered her parents. As she dropped the letter in the post box, she knew she was now cut off from Jamie even though she would be able to write to him. She felt completely alone, but it made her more determined that once she had a job and had earned enough, she and Jamie would be off on their travels.

How much, however, was enough? Rae had no idea what it would cost to go abroad.

'And so, until your father and I have decided what to do with you, Hannah-Rae, you can earn your keep by cleaning the house and taking Jack to school in the morning and picking him up in the afternoon until he breaks up, and since you seem to like gardening, you can keep ours tidy. Let's hope you can manage to do that,' Mama said at dinner that evening.

Rae began to collect snippets of information about other countries, and having bought a French language book in an old bookshop which she passed on her way to Jack's school, she carried on learning French and writing to Jamie, although she knew she wouldn't hear from him.

* * *

Mama passed her medical exam and was now working at the Royal Free Hospital, where she was carrying on with her studies to be a surgeon. Joe was still boarding at Bishop's Hall Boys' School, and Jack was keen to walk to and from school with his friends — and without Rae. The garden was scrupulously tidy, and although Rae would have been happy to work in anyone else's garden, none of their neighbours seemed to think a girl would be able to manage.

'It's time you did something meaningful, Hannah-Rae,' Mama said, and for once Rae agreed with her.

'I wondered if I could work in France as a nanny, like Thérèse did when she came here,' Rae said.

Mama seemed impressed that she had suggested something sensible, but surprisingly, Papa wasn't in favour. 'Things are too unstable on the continent at the moment,' he said. 'That aggressive little man, Hitler, seems to be doing his best to cause problems. I don't trust him. He's already invaded Czechoslovakia and got away with it. Now he's got his eye on Poland.'

The previous September, Prime Minister Neville Chamberlain had returned from Munich waving a piece of paper signed by Hitler, and to the country's relief, he'd declared he'd ensure 'peace for our time'.

She reminded Papa of the prime minister's words but still he remained doubtful about her going abroad. 'Train as a nanny and perhaps by the time you've qualified, things'll have settled down. The best place is the Norland Institute, so I should contact them, although your academic record isn't exactly impressive. But at least you can find out if it's worth applying there.'

'You should have put more effort into your lessons when you were at school and then it wouldn't be an issue,' said Mama, making it clear she doubted Rae would be accepted.

Rae sighed. She thought it unlikely she'd be accepted either, but then, it wasn't that she wanted to be a nanny. She simply wanted to work in France until Jamie could join her, and then after a while they'd move on, perhaps to Spain . . . or Italy. Each day, as well as practising French from the textbooks she'd bought in the second-hand book shop, she now pored over the newspapers, taking in everything about the situation in Europe and paying special attention to what was happening in Germany.

And then, Adolph Hitler invaded Poland.

'The man's a lunatic!' said Papa. 'It's going to mean war, you mark my words.'

War? Could it be possible?

On Sunday the third of September, at eleven fifteen, the Kingsley family gathered around their wireless in the drawing room and waited for Mr Chamberlain to make an announcement. He informed the nation that Hitler had failed to agree to withdraw his troops from Poland by eleven o'clock that morning and consequently, England was now at war with Germany.

* * *

Within minutes of the declaration of war, the air raid sirens went off. Seconds of inactivity passed while the Kingsleys struggled to take in the enormity of the announcement followed by the sudden shrill warning of danger.

Papa was used to emergencies and to reacting speedily, and he instructed everyone to take their gas masks and to follow him to the Anderson shelter which they, like many of their neighbours, had installed in the garden. As they hurried to the shelter, Rae looked up expecting to see hordes of black German bombers, like a swarm of mosquitos above them ready to drop their deadly cargo, but the sky was clear and blue.

How can we be at war? Everything looks so normal.

It turned out to be a false alarm, but the scene was set for the battle of nerves which lasted for eight months and became known as the 'Phoney War', the time when, although at war, Britain was involved in very little military action.

But despite that, all precautions had to be taken and it became second nature to ensure the blackout curtains didn't allow light through, to carry a gas mask at all times, and for many children to be evacuated to rural areas that were considered safer than London and the big cities and ports.

It was like being out at sea in a boat with no rudder that was completely at the mercy of the winds, thought Rae. Travel was out of the question, and training to be a nanny seemed pointless until the war was over. She was simply drifting.

Rae had written Jamie lots of letters telling him all about Chelsea and had said that he could write to her because she no longer worried that it would anger Mama and Papa. It was rare for either of her parents to beat her to the post deliveries each day, so it was unlikely they'd find out he'd written. But so far, she'd only received one picture postcard in an envelope from him explaining he was very busy working in his uncle's yard and helping his cousin, Duncan, in his cockle fishing business. The photograph on the card showed the grand entrance pavilion into the Kursaal amusement park in Southend. Jamie had drawn two snails and next to them, a compass showing they were heading east. *Us*, he'd written over the snails with a large arrow, as if by making his intentions even clearer, they might come true sooner.

The Kursaal was a special place to them. The ticket seller on the Caterpillar Ride had been the catalyst to them discovering how they felt about each other, and Rae often wondered what might have happened if Jamie had simply escorted her home believing she hadn't wanted to be with him and if she'd believed he hadn't wanted to be with her. But fate, in the form of the ticket seller, had intervened. One day fate would help them again, and when the war was over, like the snails, they'd both head east — together.

★   ★   ★

1940

By May, the news from Europe had gone from bad to worse. Hitler had invaded Denmark and Norway and launched his *Blitzkrieg* — Lightning War, against Belgium and Holland. At home, Prime Minister Chamberlain resigned and was replaced by Winston Churchill.

By mid-May, the BBC announced that the admiralty wanted all owners of self-propelled craft between thirty and a hundred feet to send particulars within fourteen days so that the boats could be requisitioned.

'Well, the *Lady Amelia*'s escaped then,' Papa said. 'If she was four feet longer, she'd have qualified.'

'That would've been a shame,' said Rae. 'We've only taken her out once ourselves. What d'you think the admiralty wants the boats for? Surely the navy have ships of their own.'

'I'm not sure, but I've got a friend in the admiralty and he said things are looking bad for our boys in France and Belgium, although it's rather hush-hush at the moment. It sounds like the navy might have to go to pick up troops, but if they're calling for small boats to help, the situation must be desperate.'

Just after Rae had been sent home from school, Jamie's father, Robert MacKenzie, had informed Papa that he was closing his boatyard at Chichester Harbour. Alex had joined the RAF and Jamie was needed in Leigh, so although when he'd started the business he'd intended to leave it to his sons, they were no longer there. Of course, one or indeed both sons might return to the boatyard one day, but Mr MacKenzie couldn't wait and he closed up and retired. He suggested that since the Kingsley family were moving to London, it would be better to move *Wild Spirit* to Leigh where his brother Gordon could look after it.

Papa had taken a few days' leave from the hospital and he, Jack and Rae had sailed the small dinghy around the coast to Essex. When they'd arrived in Leigh, Gordon MacKenzie had proudly shown them his boatyard, but to Rae's deep disappointment, Jamie had been out cockle fishing with his cousin.

Papa had spotted a twenty-six-foot motor yacht being built and had enquired about the cost. *Wild Spirit* was a wonderful boat for his children, but he hankered after something large enough for all the family.

'As it happens, that one's for sale,' Gordon said. 'The new owner died before taking possession. I'd be happy to come to some arrangement.'

Since then, Rae and Papa had been out on *Lady Amelia* once, on a trip to Whitstable in Kent. And now with the war on, it looked like it would be a long time before they would have the opportunity to sail her again.

Days after the BBC's announcement, Papa telephoned from the hospital.

'Hello, poppet. Listen, I've got to get back to work, but I wondered if I could trust you with a job.'

'Yes, Papa?'

'Gordon MacKenzie at Leigh has telephoned to say the Ministry of Shipping has contacted him about any small boats they have or may know about. He had to tell them about the *Lady Amelia* and they're going to requisition it.'

'But I thought they wanted boats of thirty feet or more?'

'They did, but now they're after smaller boats as well. So d'you think you could go down to Leigh, unlock the cabin, and get all our personal things off the boat before it's taken? I'd rather the lock wasn't broken, and I've got an old compass Grandad gave me in the drawer that I'd hate to lose. D'you mind, poppet?'

'I don't mind, Papa, but I think Mama might.'

'Leave her to me. I know you're referring to the possibility of running into Jamie MacKenzie, but you seem to be growing up since you've been home and I've never had a problem with Jamie, anyway. He's a nice lad. But just don't tell your mother I said that! I thought perhaps Joanna wouldn't mind if you stayed there one night. I could ring and ask. I'm a bit worried about you being held up on the train and being out after blackout.'

'I don't think Mama would like that. Joanna's *her* cousin. But I could ask Ada Quinn. She said I could sleep there when I like and if you don't mind, I could stay for a week and do a bit of work on her garden while I'm there, to thank her for letting me stay.'

'Shall I telephone her to ask?' Papa said.

'No, Papa; she doesn't have a telephone. But don't worry. She won't mind if I simply turn up.'

★   ★   ★

Rae dressed in warm clothes suitable for sailing. With any luck, she'd have a chance to take *Lady Amelia* out with Jamie before it was requisitioned, and if not, perhaps they'd be able to take out *Wild Spirit*. But more than anything, Rae hoped Jamie would simply be there.

Fenchurch Street Station was busier than Rae had ever seen it, with many uniformed people milling about. There were so many changes. Train windows were covered in black paint so that at night no light would spill out of the carriages, and the passengers seemed to be friendlier than before the war, chatting about food shortages, the film on at the local cinema, success or failure in battles, and how they were coping with the war so far.

Rae had been to Leigh-on-Sea several times with Jamie and remembered it as a sleepy little fishing village. It didn't occur to her that anything would be different from those occasions, so she was surprised to see so many people get off at the station and even more surprised to be stopped by a policeman at the ticket barrier wanting to see her identity card and to know what business she had in Leigh. When she told him she was volunteering her father's boat to the admiralty, he let her pass and she slipped through the bustling crowds of fishermen, naval officers and ratings, and headed down to the water front, her anxiety growing. This was nothing like she'd imagined. There'd been newspaper reports about countries falling to the German army and ships being sunk, but they all seemed rather remote. Now she was surrounded by uniformed men, and for the first time since the start of the war it felt very real. And very threatening.

She flattened herself against a wall as a group of naval officers walked along the narrow High Street, talking animatedly, heedless of her presence. What was she doing here? This wasn't a game. What had she been thinking when she imagined she might go sailing with Jamie if she could find him? The situation here was serious.

'Rae?'

She looked up. Jamie stepped out of the crowd and was next to her, shaking his head in disbelief.

'Oh, Jamie!' Rae threw her arms around his neck and held him tightly, not only because she was thrilled to see him but because she was afraid.

He led her by the hand to the gate of his uncle's boatyard and into the small office.

'Rae, what are you doing here?'

She explained and he nodded. 'Let's go. You might find they've already broken the lock and are aboard. But they might not have got to it yet. Come on.'

Jamie held her hand, plying her with questions as they hurried along the waterfront towards the *Lady Amelia*.

Nobody from the admiralty had yet claimed her, and after unlocking the cabin, Rae took out all the personal items she could find, including her grandad's compass.

'It's so good to see you, Rae,' Jamie said. 'I've missed you so much. The only thing that keeps me going is the belief that one day we'll be able to set off together. North, south, east or west, I don't care which way so long as you're with me.' He paused. 'You do still want that, don't you?'

'Of course! If only the war would be over.'

'I know,' said Jamie, 'but the news from France isn't good.'

'They'll pick up our men all right, won't they?'

'I don't know. Apparently there're thousands of them trapped on the coast. That's what all these navy people are doing here.'

Rae's mouth dropped open. 'Thousands?' It all started making sense — the requisitioning of large and then small boats.

'Don't worry, we'll get them back. We're setting off shortly.' He checked his watch. 'I'd better go. Duncan's taking his cockle boat.'

Rae held him tightly. 'You said *we*. You're not going, are you?'

'Of course!'

'No, Jamie! Isn't this a navy operation?'

He shook his head and unclasped her hands from around his neck. 'No, they need small boats with a shallow draught to go to the beaches to lift off our men. I can help, Rae. I can do something to try to get this war over. I need to go now. Take your things and get back to Ada's — this is no place for you.'

Ada had let Walter go . . . and she'd never seen him again, thought Rae. She caught hold of Jamie's jacket. 'If you're going, I'm going with you!'

'Rae, you can't! Duncan won't take you for a start. And if you don't let me go now, he'll leave without me.'

'Then let's take the Lady Amelia. At least that way I can be with you. I'm a better sailor than you any day!'

'It's too dangerous, Rae! No! Go home; I'll come and find you when I get back. I promise. I'll let you know as soon as I'm safe.'

Rae shook her head, 'No. I couldn't bear it. I'm coming with you, and if you won't let me, I'll go on my own!'

'Rae, don't be ridiculous. You can't go alone.'

'Then I'll volunteer to go on another boat.' She took her father's knitted hat out of her bag and pulled it on, tucking her shoulder-length curls inside. She wouldn't pass as a man but she could conceivably pass as a boy.

'If things are as desperate as you say, I'll get on a boat one way or another. I'm a fine sailor. I'll be useful. And if anyone finds out I'm a girl and objects to me being there, we'll be at sea. And if they turn back, well, I'll just have to put up with it. But I'm going to give it a go!'

★　★　★

Seeing her determination, Jamie had given in and decided he'd rather be with Rae in the *Lady Amelia*, although she knew he was hoping she wouldn't be allowed to go. But in the end, it had been remarkably easy. She'd signed on as 'Ray Kingsley' and if anyone suspected she wasn't a boy, they weren't interested.

With great speed and efficiency, blankets and fresh water were loaded into the *Lady Amelia*, and the engines fuelled. Sidney Fuller, the naval rating who'd been assigned to take charge of the *Lady Amelia*, was calm and professional, and if he was nervous about the trip, he didn't display any apprehension to Rae and Jamie.

When Rae thought about it later, the fact that no one had bothered to take a closer look at her or attempted to dissuade her should have rung alarm bells. But it didn't. She had no idea how desperate the endeavour, which Sidney referred to as Operation Dynamo, was.

The *Lady Amelia* followed the fishing and cockle vessels out of Leigh and then joined the tugs which had come from London and now poured out of the Thames on their way down to Ramsgate, where after refuelling, the long trip across to Dunkirk would begin.

'We'll follow the channels that've been swept,' Sidney announced cheerfully. He was a sandy-haired man a few years older than Jamie and appeared to take everything in his stride. 'Swept of mines,' he added, noticing Rae's puzzled expression.

The sea conditions were perfect. 'Just like a mill pond,' Sidney said with satisfaction. 'Don't suppose there's any chance of a cuppa, Ray?'

To Rae's surprise, Jamie followed her below into the cabin.

He held his fingers to his lips. 'I don't know if you realise how dangerous this is, but just in case . . . just in case . . . one of us . . . one of us doesn't make it back, I want to tell you something,' he whispered. 'I love you Rae. I always have, right from the first time I laid eyes on you. And if we make it back alive, I'll do whatever it takes to be with you . . . if you want me.'

She'd known he loved her, but this was the first time he'd ever told her.

Rae threw her arms around his neck, 'Of course I want you, Jamie. I love you too.' It was the first time she'd told him.

Jamie kissed his two fingers, but she caught his hand before he could touch her lips. 'No, kiss me properly, Jamie.'

She put her hands behind his head and pulling his face towards hers, closing her eyes.

For a second he hesitated, but she could feel his breath on her cheek and she pulled him even closer. As his lips brushed hers, she shivered and he drew back in alarm.

'Rae?' he whispered.

'Kiss me again,' she said and before he could answer, she covered his mouth with hers, pressing her body against his. How could she not have known that kissing Jamie would be so right? How could she not have realised their bodies would fit together so perfectly?

She clung to him, feeling his lips pressing hers and tasting him. Why had she waited until now, until they were both in danger, to show him how much she wanted him?

Tears slipped down her cheeks, and detecting the saltiness, he drew back. 'Rae?' She knew he was afraid their kiss had raised memories she wanted to forget.

'I love you, Jamie, and I wish I'd

kissed you before.'

He smiled at her with relief and they stood, their foreheads touching, holding each other.

A thud on the door to the cabin made them both jump. 'Ray, are you boiling the water over a match?' Sidney called. 'I'm parched. Get a move on!'

* * *

As they drew closer to the French coast, more and more ships and small boats were visible, all heading in the same direction.

'This is unbelievable,' whispered Rae, a shiver of pride and fear running down her spine at the scale of Operation Dynamo. But surely someone in the admiralty had made a mistake? Someone must have underestimated how many people would respond to their call, because such an enormous number of boats couldn't all be needed to rescue soldiers. Most would go back to England empty, Rae was sure.

Gradually they sailed into a sea mist. It was so light as to seem like smoke, but as they sailed on, it thickened until even the closest boats appeared ghostly and unreal. The slap of the sea against the *Lady Amelia*'s hull and the clanking of halyards on neighbouring boats were strangely muted by the fog, making it hard to pinpoint the source of sounds. But they could scarcely get lost with so many boats heading in the same direction.

Sidney wasn't disturbed by the lack of visibility. 'It makes it a bit trickier for us, but much harder for the Germans. At least the Stukas won't take off in this weather. If the fog lifts, we might have problems.'

Stukas! Rae had read about the Junkers Stuka German dive-bombers that screamed as they descended through the sky to shoot and to drop their destructive payload, but it hadn't occurred to her they might be firing and bombing the fleet of civilian rescue ships. She longed to hold Jamie's hand to take comfort from him, but she didn't want Sidney to see, so she simply looked out at the sea, keeping watch for anything in their path. Sidney said the mine sweepers had already cleared their path, but in this fog who could tell?

Soon they began to pass Royal Navy cruisers and destroyers at anchor. The water was no longer deep enough for them to proceed, and they were waiting for the small boats to go to the shore and bring the stranded soldiers to them.

They still couldn't see the shore because of the fog, which had become denser and blacker. An acrid smell of burning oil filled their nostrils, and Rae realised it was the smoke from fires which was mixing with the fog, smothering them in a thick blanket. The crack of gunfire and boom of exploding shells drifted across the water from the direction in which they were heading, and gradually Rae began to make out tiny pinpricks of red light like sequins in the gloom.

'That's Dunkirk,' said Sidney. 'The Germans've pretty much destroyed it.'

'How can we land there?' Jamie asked.

'We're not going to. We've got a shallow draught, so our orders are to head for the beaches. We'll get as close as we can, load up with men, and then ferry them to one of the larger ships that can't get any closer. Then we do it again. And again . . . until there are no more men or we die in the effort.'

Sidney sounded relaxed, as if he were proposing a day boating on a lake, but Rae could see the lines of tension around his mouth and knew he was more concerned than he appeared. While Sidney was preoccupied with the wheel, Rae placed her hand next to Jamie's on the side of the boat. She wanted to touch him, to make contact, to feel his warmth. Without saying anything, Jamie slid his hand over hers and squeezed, then just as quickly removed it when Sidney turned to look at them.

The fog began to lift as they approached

the wide expanse of beach, and Rae couldn't believe the sight opening up in front of her. Queues of men snaked from the water's edge to the dunes at the back of the beach, as far as she could see in either direction, looking like orderly lines of ants moving forward when a boat approached them. But as soon as the men were taken from the front, they were replaced by more, in what seemed to be a never-ending supply of soldiers.

Suddenly from above there was an ear-splitting scream as a Stuka dived out of the sky, with a rat-tat-tat of its guns as it strafed the sand. At the sound of the eerie shrieking of the dive-bomber and its machine gunfire, the men in the queues dived for cover, lying flat on the beach as the hail of bullets threw up bursts of sand. When the plane had gone, the men stood up, dusted themselves down, and once again took up their places in the orderly if meandering queues.

Sidney steered the *Lady Amelia*

towards the beach, stopping some way from the shoreline.

'That's as close as we get. It shelves from here, so they'll have to come out to us,' he said, and cupping his hands around his mouth, he shouted to the officer at the head of the closest queue to send out a dozen men without their weapons. The officer pushed twelve men into the water towards the boat, and those behind shuffled forward to fill their places, enviously watching the men wade out, first up to their knees, then their waists and finally their chests.

Rae and Jamie reached out to their eager hands and pulled them aboard, pointing out where to sit, so their weight was distributed equally. When the three weakest soldiers had been taken below and the others arranged on the deck, many with their dripping legs dangling over the side of the boat while they held on to the stanchions, Sidney turned and headed out towards one of the larger boats.

Suddenly panic broke out on the shore,

and several men rushed past their officer towards the *Lady Amelia* and clung on to the legs of the men on deck, trying to pull themselves up on to the boat, which began to list dangerously.

'Get them off or we'll capsize!' Sidney yelled, and opening the throttle, he turned and headed out to sea, leaving all but one, who still clung on until they'd gone about a two hundred yards; then he too, fell off and sank beneath the surface.

'We can't just leave him!' said Rae.

'He's gone. Most likely drowned,' Sidney said calmly, following Jamie and Rae's line of gaze. 'It's a shame, but we have to think of these lads now. It seems they haven't had clean water for days, Jamie. Perhaps you and Ray would get them a drink.'

After transferring the weary men to a navy ship, Sidney turned around and set out for the shore. 'Well, that's the first dozen as safe as we can make them, now back to get more. By my reckoning, we're going to be making quite a few more trips before we make a dent in that lot on the beach.'

His words were casual and detached, but he gripped the helm tightly, and Rae could see he, too, was daunted by the task ahead of them. They made their way back to the beach to pick up their human cargo going in the same direction as many of the other tiny, assorted boats and passing others, full of men, sailing in the opposite direction, towards a larger ship, ready to offload theirs.

The fog had lifted completely and the Stukas were back, bombing the ships, strafing the beaches and causing utter panic with their devilish screams as they swooped out of the skies.

I have to keep my mind on the job. I must focus, Rae told herself when she saw a ferry steamer further out to sea take a direct hit. Men jumped into the water as it sank with astonishing speed. All those soldiers had just been rescued from the beach by small craft such as the *Lady Amelia*.

For what?

To believe they'd reached safety and then to have the ship blown out from under them was too cruel.

Rae had never felt so helpless.

On their third trip back to the beach, they saw a Stuka swoop down, his bullets making successive bursts of sand and then splashes in the sea as his sights followed the lines of men. One of the soldiers who was wading out to the *Lady Amelia* was obviously hit, and a sergeant who was standing next to him caught him, lifted him on to his shoulders and carried him towards the boat. By the time he reached the *Lady Amelia*, he was up to his shoulders in water and his strength was obviously failing.

'What are you doing?' Rae asked as Jamie took off his boots.

'I'll help the wounded man in. You grab his arms, Rae!' Jamie said as he climbed over the side and landed in the sea with a splash.

'Jamie! No!'

But it was too late.

Jamie helped the sergeant push the injured man up towards Rae, who hauled him onboard; then Sidney dragged him below to one of the bunks. Meanwhile, other soldiers clambered on to the deck and pulled the sergeant up.

Jamie was still shoulder-deep in the water, and Rae reached out to take his hand to help him aboard, but the Stuka had turned and was heading straight for them, preceded by rapid machine-gun fire that sent up a shower of spray as each bullet hit the water. The *Lady Amelia* lurched as Sidney tried to surge forward out of the line of gunfire, throwing two men from the deck into the water and knocking Rae off her feet. She scrambled up as the boat turned, and looked back at Jamie. His head was still visible and she saw him touch his fingers to his lips, raising them up as a salute to her before he disappeared beneath the wash caused by the sudden acceleration of the *Lady Amelia*.

'Get down!' Sidney yelled to Rae,

and one of the soldiers reached up and pulled her to the deck. As the German pilot veered the Stuka sharply and came in for another attack, Sidney turned hard on the wheel, wildly swinging the boat around away from the salvo, as men gripped on to anything within reach. With her face pressed to the deck, Rae felt the impact of the bullets tearing through wood and scrambled to her knees to see how much damage had been done. The Luftwaffe pilot carried on, perhaps more interested in larger targets or perhaps believing he'd done enough damage to sink the boat, and flew back towards land.

Miraculously, the bullets had hit the deck but didn't seem to have damaged the hull, and as far as she could tell, the boat was still seaworthy.

'Turn around! We've got to fetch Jamie' Rae shouted above the scream of the Stuka and the noise of the bullets spraying several other nearby boats.

'No, we need to drop these men off first.'

'But we have to go back! We can't just leave him!' Rae grabbed Sidney by the arm, and it was then she saw the blood on his jacket.

'You've been hit!'

'It's nothing,' Sidney said calmly, 'but we're not going back. Not until these men are safe. They've already suffered enough.' His expression was resolute.

'You can't leave Jamie there!'

But Rae knew he wouldn't turn back.

For a second, she considered jumping overboard and swimming back to Jamie, but if he'd been hit, she wouldn't have been able to help him. His only hope was if they returned to pick him up in the *Lady Amelia*.

Sidney set a course for a large naval vessel and Rae told herself that when they'd unloaded the men, they'd be able to go back to the beach and find Jamie; but as they drew nearer to the ship, there was a sudden roar and an explosion.

'It's hit a mine! Hold on!' Sidney shouted and turned the helm to head into the huge wave that was spreading out from the stricken ship rather than to take its full force sideways-on. Within minutes, the large ship had sunk beneath the bubbling surface, leaving men bobbing like corks in its wake.

'Why're you sailing away from them?' Rae asked, expecting him to head towards the men.

'Where would we put them?' Sidney asked. 'If we take more on board, we're likely to sink.' He clung to the wheel and Rae began to wonder if his wound was worse than he'd previously admitted.

'We're heading home,' he announced, and the men cheered. Then he added quietly to Rae, 'If anything should happen to me, you're in charge. Can you handle it, Ray?'

Rae nodded.

'We need to make sure the men have confidence in us. Understood?'

'Yes.'

'So, not a word about my wound.'

Rae nodded. 'Is there anything I can do to help?'

'Make sure they've all had something to drink. And keep their spirits up.'

Sidney remained at the helm until Ramsgate was in sight.

'Over to you,' he said to Rae and then he passed out, his sleeve drenched in blood.

Rae took the wheel and steered into the harbour.

6

The memorial for the Leigh-on-Sea fishermen and cocklemen who'd lost their lives at Dunkirk was held at St Clement's Church in Leigh. Not only Jamie and his cousin Duncan had been lost, but one of the cockle boats, *Renown*, and its crew of four had been blown up by a mine.

Rae took the train from London to the coast on her own. Papa had wanted to join her but the influx of soldiers, airmen and sailors who'd been involved in Operation Dynamo was stretching the medical services, and he and Mama were spending more and more time at work, even sleeping in their respective hospitals when they weren't on duty.

St Clement's Church was packed; almost everyone in Leigh was related to or knew at least one of the victims, and the silence in the church and the collective grief were almost too hard for Rae to bear.

After the service, Jamie's Uncle Gordon stopped her as she was leaving. 'I'm so sorry, lass . . . ' He faltered and she could see him fighting to keep back the tears.

She nodded, also unable to speak. What was there to say? He'd lost a nephew and a son.

'You!' It was Jamie's father, Robert MacKenzie. His eyes were blazing. 'I always knew you were trouble! I knew in the end you'd hurt my lad. I had no idea you'd get him killed!'

'Robert,' Gordon said, stepping between his brother and Rae, 'stop! Don't you think the lass's been through enough?'

Jamie's father was shaking with rage, his fists clenching and unclenching and his lip curled in contempt. 'She's not been through enough! She hasn't lost a son. She just played with Jamie. He was just a toy. She's just a spoiled, rich brat!'

Rae pushed past Gordon, and raising

her chin, she said slowly, 'I loved Jamie. And I'm sorry you feel that way about me. But I truly loved him and I always will.' She turned and walked away.

Gordon ran after her. 'Don't take any notice, lass. He always was hot-headed. He doesn't mean it. But you're always welcome in my house.'

It was just as well Papa hadn't come. Not only would he have witnessed Robert MacKenzie's outburst, but he would also have discovered his daughter had been on the *Lady Amelia* with Jamie when it had sailed to Dunkirk, a detail that so far Rae had told no one. There hadn't been any point in telling her parents. Of course, they knew Jamie had not returned and they'd put her distress and emotional fragility down to his death.

But there was no point telling them what had really happened. It was all in the past and there was nothing they could do about it now. And if they tried to punish her, there was nothing they could do that would have touched her in the slightest. Rae was in too much pain already. She'd learned a terrible lesson and had no intention of getting in any more trouble. Papa may have once believed she had a wild spirit, but those days were over.

Rae had no more spirit left.

★　★　★

September, 1940

On Saturday the seventh of September, unusually, all of the Kingsley family were at home together enjoying the late summer sunshine when air raid sirens began to wail. It was almost five o'clock. Wave after wave of Luftwaffe bombers had crossed the Channel and were travelling towards London, where they were about to target the docks in the east.

That night, the raging fires in the East London Docks guided more German bomber pilots who carried on bombarding the capital, killing, maiming, and destroying buildings.

The following evening, the Germans returned to continue their aerial attack.

'I'm going to ask Joanna if she wouldn't mind having Jack and Rae for a while,' Mama said. 'At least until they stop bombing London. I can't concentrate on work when I know they're home here. And spending all night in the Anderson shelter's so uncomfortable. At least in Essex they should be safe.'

Papa agreed.

Joe, who'd volunteered for the RAF and was about to be stationed at Hornchurch, accompanied Rae and Jack to Laindon Station to meet Joanna and to stay at Priory Hall for a few days.

Rae expected Joanna to bring Faye to meet them at Laindon and perhaps even Mark, but she was surprised to see two other girls waiting with them outside the station. And even more surprised to learn that although Joanna had just met the two girls, she'd invited them to stay at Priory Hall.

Apparently the two sisters, Miriam and Rebekah, had arrived in England after being brought out of Germany on a Kindertransport train. They were German Jews who'd escaped the Nazi regime after losing their parents in a bomb blast.

Rae and Miriam immediately took to each other despite being different temperamentally. Rae loved to work with the Land Army girls on Ben's farm and had tried to persuade Miriam to join her, but she was not as strong as Rae and preferred to help Joanna with Mark and Faye and to remain indoors. Nevertheless, Rae identified with the German girl, recognising that they both felt displaced, as if they didn't belong anywhere.

And where Rae was mourning Jamie, she felt that Miriam was also secretly grieving for something or someone. But after learning some of the two German girls' experiences, she didn't pry. If Miriam wanted to tell her, she would do so in her own time, and Rae would be there to listen. Perhaps one day she'd tell Miriam about Jamie and the last time she'd seen him.

But not yet.

be there to listen. Perhaps one day she'd tell Miriam about Jamie and the feelings

7

Jamie often woke at night in his prison cell, his mind filled with images from that terrible day when he'd stood shoulder-deep in the water next to the beach near Dunkirk.

He remembered the stench of burning oil, the screams of men and Stukas, the explosion of shells and the rat-a-tat-tat of gunfire. And he recalled the impact of the bullet that had hit him in the leg. The water had slowed the bullet down and it had only grazed his thigh, but it had been enough to tear into his flesh.

At first, the shock of seeing the *Lady Amelia* sailing away had numbed his mind and he barely noticed that he'd been wounded. He'd watched as the boat zigzagged in an effort to avoid the bullets. The men had all thrown themselves to the deck to try to avoid the strafing — but not Rae. She'd stood with her arm outstretched towards him. He'd sent her a kiss and hoped she'd seen. And then the same pilot who'd hit him had swooped over the *Lady Amelia*, and Jamie had heard bullets tearing into wood and he knew they'd been hit. His view had been obliterated by soldiers who were surging towards a tugboat that had just arrived, and then there was a terrible explosion and water was hurled into the air.

He guessed it was a mine.

When the tugboat pulled away laden with men, Jamie's view was unimpeded and he could see the stern of an enormous ship pointing up to the sky with men floating around it, grabbing on to debris to keep on the surface. The *Lady Amelia*, however, could no longer be seen.

Had it already sunk?

He stared out to sea, unable to believe what had just happened; and then as a huge wave was about to engulf him, someone grabbed him and hauled him onto a boat. As he was dragged on board, pain shot through his leg and he realised he'd been wounded. After that, he must have passed out because he couldn't remember anything.

Later, he regained consciousness and found he was on a boat with French soldiers. One of them introduced himself as Jean-Jacques Pierlot, telling Jamie in heavily accented English that they would soon arrive at their destination.

'Ramsgate?' Jamie asked with relief.

Jean-Jacques laughed. 'Ramsgate? No, we are not going to England. We will soon arrive in Normandy.'

Jean-Jacques had taken Jamie to his parents' farmhouse, a remote stone building not far from the coast. Monsieur and Madame Pierlot didn't speak English but were very welcoming and were obviously thrilled to have their son return.

'They say the Germans are on their way,' Jean-Jacques said. 'Panzer divisions and infantry. We must hide until we can contact the Resistance, and then we will try to get you home.'

Madame Pierlot led Jean-Jacques and Jamie into the stone cellar, where she made up two beds on straw mattresses and brought them food.

'Until the Germans arrive,' Jean-Jacques said, 'my mother will leave the trapdoor open. But once the Bosche come, you must stay down here until we know how life is going to be. They may leave us alone . . . or they may not. I am going out tonight to try to contact anyone who is working for the Resistance.'

During the night, Jamie awoke feeling very hot and thirsty. That was strange, he thought, because earlier he'd noticed the cellar was cold and damp. And his thigh hurt. It felt as though it was going to burst.

He lost track of time after that, although the trapdoor had been closed, so he suspected the Germans had arrived and were now occupying this part of Normandy. Presumably they had marched through and were on their way to the far reaches of France. From time to time, someone wiped the sweat from his face with a cool cloth and held water to his lips, although on one occasion he felt a hand clamp over his mouth but was too weak to push it away. Above, he could hear stamping on the floor. Or perhaps they were Germans marching about wearing boots, because the man with the hand over his mouth was saying, 'Shh, shh! The Bosche are here,' quietly in his ear.

One day — or perhaps night; it was hard to tell once the trapdoor was closed — Jamie woke with a clear head. His leg was bandaged and it hurt when he moved it, but at least the fever had broken.

When Jean-Jacques appeared with a lantern some time later, he was relieved to find Jamie a little better. 'Two British agents will arrive soon and we will find a way to get you home,' he said, 'but you must get well first. You must be able to walk.'

Madame Pierlot brought Jamie food and sat with him while he ate, speaking slowly in French. Gradually he picked up words and phrases, remembering things that he'd learned from books years before but had never known how to pronounce.

Two Special Operations Executive agents were due to arrive during the early hours of Sunday morning. Madame Pierlot wound fresh bandages tightly around his leg, and although it was painful, he was able to walk fairly quickly with the aid of a stick.

Jamie and Jean-Jacques left the Pierlots' farmhouse at midnight. That gave them plenty of time to get to the improvised airfield ready to meet the other members of the Resistance and the airplane containing two agents, bomb-making equipment, and a precious radio transmitter.

It was hard to make out the small black Lysander airplane against the night sky, but the sound of its engines was unmistakable and the Resistance members flashed a signal with torches to guide it in. It descended and when the wheels touched down, it bumped across the grass, coming to a standstill not far from where Jamie was waiting.

Just as the door opened, a searchlight beam cut through the darkness with shocking brilliance. From behind the Resistance fighters, rifles clicked, and a German officer strutted out from the bushes followed by a dozen soldiers who fanned out, crouched and took aim at the airplane and those gathered nearby.

Everyone was quickly rounded up, and with their hands on their heads, they were marched to a vehicle parked some way off and loaded in the back with two armed guards. Jamie now knew enough French to understand one of the Resistance fighters whispering to another that someone must have betrayed them. That seemed likely because it was obvious the Germans hadn't simply stumbled across them — they'd been waiting in position.

'Who?' the other man whispered in reply, and then Jamie heard Jean-Jacques's name mentioned, followed by a rapid burst of French Jamie couldn't follow. Surely they didn't suspect Jean-Jacques? Jamie looked around for him. There were the two British agents, a man and a woman, as well as the RAF pilot and four members of the Resistance, but Jean-Jacques was missing.

'Quiet!' one of the guards shouted at the two Frenchmen, raising his gun.

They were driven to the police station in town which the Germans had taken over, and placed in cells. One by one, they were taken for interrogation by the commanding officer, and when it was Jamie's turn, he told the truth about coming over on a small boat to Dunkirk, only keeping back the name of the Pierlots. After all, he knew nothing other than that. He didn't even know the name of the town he was now in, much less the location of the remote farmhouse. The officer blenched when he saw Jamie's wound and ordered it to be dressed by his medical officer.

'It smells,' he said, wrinkling his nose. 'Take him away. We do not need young, foolish English civilians. Bring me the female agent.'

When Jamie was once more on his own, he wondered about Jean-Jacques. Surely he wouldn't have taken Jamie in only to betray him. But it seemed the others in the Resistance believed that to be the case. Jean-Jacques had volunteered to take up position on his own at the bottom of the field so he could indicate the end of the makeshift runway to the pilot of the Lysander. If he was collaborating with the Germans, that would have been the perfect position to make a quick getaway while the others were taken prisoner.

Jamie shared a cell with two of the Resistance fighters, both of whom regarded him with suspicion since he'd been living with Jean-Jacques. One morning, both of them were taken away and didn't return. When the guard came with his food, Jamie used gestures to ask where the others had gone, and the German silently drew an imaginary line across his neck with his finger.

Jamie lost track of time after the others disappeared. Day after day he remained alone. It seemed the commanding officer had believed his story and recognised that Jamie had no interesting information for the Germans, and therefore was of no value at all.

It appeared as if he'd been completely forgotten.

* * *

One morning, the guard came into the cell and gestured that Jamie was leaving.

'Where am I going?' Jamie asked, his hands palms up to try to indicate that he was asking a question.

He expected the guard to reply with a shrug as usual, but this time he said, 'Deutschland. To work.'

He looked doubtfully at Jamie, whose leg had still not healed and who'd weakened after his fever and the time spent in prison with very little food. Then he shrugged.

Jamie was loaded onto a truck, and seconds later the two British agents were bundled into the back with him, followed by two armed guards.

The agents looked surprised to see Jamie. 'Firing squad too?' the man asked, his face a swollen mass of bruises.

'Silence!' roared one of the guards.

Jamie looked at the two agents and realised how lucky he'd been — so far, at least. The woman had also been mistreated, presumably in an attempt to get information out of her. But now, if they were facing the firing squad, why was Jamie in the truck with them? Had the guard been wrong when he said Jamie was going to be sent to Germany to work?

Jamie knew they'd left the town because the road surface became slightly more uneven and he could no longer see houses and roofs, just the sky, through the small area between the high tailgate and the canvas cover over the top of the truck. Trees began to appear, indicating they were travelling through a wooded area which had sharp bends that threw the passengers in the back from side to side. Suddenly the brakes were applied with such force that they were all hurled forwards, and before the guards in the back could recover their balance, men wearing balaclavas had scaled the tailgate, guns pointing into the interior of the truck.

The driver and guards were dragged out and disarmed, then led into the forest by one of the masked men while one of the others climbed into the driving seat and turned the truck around. As soon as the masked man had returned from the woods and climbed into the passenger seat, they drove back towards the town, and when they were moving at speed, the men removed their balaclavas.

Jamie only recognised one of the men — it was Jean-Jacques. And they greeted each other warmly.

'I am sorry we couldn't get to you sooner, Jamie,' he said. 'It has not been easy to establish a new Resistance network, but I think we have a good team now.'

At the crossroads, the truck turned right, in the opposite direction to the town, and headed through narrow country lanes towards the coast.

Finally, the driver pulled off the road and headed down a rutted path, then crept slowly into a large barn. The doors were closed behind it, hiding the truck from any German pilots who might be flying overhead, and eager hands helped the agents and Jamie out.

'We wait here until it is dark,' Jean-Jacques said. 'Then hopefully two more agents arrive by boat and you will all return.'

While they waited, his men handed out bread, cheese and wine to the agents and to Jamie. Jean-Jacques explained that the Germans had known in advance about the air drop, not because someone in their network had betrayed them but because the Germans had broken the code the British Special Operations Executive was using. Once it became clear that the Germans were intercepting messages from the British to the

French Resistance, the coding system had been changed, and now it was hoped the Germans were completely unaware of the agents who would arrive later that night.

★ ★ ★

On reaching Southampton, Jamie was taken straight to hospital. After being half-starved in prison for months, the rich cheese and wine had been too much for him and with the motion of the rough seas, he'd experienced sea sickness for the first time ever, making the trip extremely uncomfortable. The wound in his leg had broken open after the unaccustomed activity, and it was later found to be infected with material from his trousers which the bullet had forced into his flesh.

While he convalesced, he dictated letters to a nurse for his father and for Rae, and she carefully wrote his words, then promised to post them for him. However, after a week there was no reply, so Jamie asked her to write to Uncle Gordon. Still there was no response, and he began to wonder if the letters had reached anyone.

It seemed like he was completely alone in the world. And if that was true, what was the point of putting all his energy into recovering?

But under the care of the doctors and nurses, the wound showed signs of beginning to heal properly, and as soon as Jamie could walk with a stick, he decided to discharge himself, much to matron's disapproval.

'I've been away from home too long,' Jamie said. 'I need to find out what's happened to everyone.'

I'll be fine, he told himself. After all, the journey from Southampton to his father's cottage wouldn't take very long, and if he was too tired, he'd stay overnight and regain his strength. But surely travelling by train wasn't going to be too taxing.

He soon discovered why his father hadn't replied to his letter when he arrived at the empty cottage. The lady from next door told him that his father had married again and was now living with his new wife. When she read the address out from her address book, Jamie laughed. His father had finally come to his senses and married Aunt Lily!

He hadn't anticipated a detour to the village where Aunt Lily lived, so by the time she and his father had got over their shock and insisted he eat with them, it was late, and they pressed him to spend the night with them.

'Of course, you're welcome to stay for more than one night,' Robert MacKenzie said. 'We'd like you to think of this as your home, too.'

Jamie was grateful to spend the night, but the following day he wanted to get to London to look for Rae. At least he knew she'd returned safely, because his father admitted he'd been very unfair to her at the memorial service.

'When you find the lass,' Robert said, 'please apologise to her for my rudeness. I had no right to speak to her like that. It was the grief speaking.'

The following morning, Aunt Lily insisted on preparing a large breakfast before he left. 'We've got to put some meat back on those bones,' she said, shaking her head sadly at his emaciated body.

She'd warned him that London had been badly hit by the Luftwaffe, but even so, he wasn't prepared for the devastation he found when he finally arrived. His earlier optimism on finding that Rae had returned from the trip to Dunkirk now turned to fear as he wondered if she'd survived that hell only to be bombed in her own home.

But to his relief, the Kingsleys' house in Chelsea was unscathed.

An elderly woman opened the door when he knocked. 'Yes?' she said, glancing over her shoulder.

'I wonder if I could see Rae, please.'

'No, sorry, she's not here.' The woman started to close the door.

'Please,' Jamie said, 'can you tell me when she'll be back?'

'No idea. I'm sorry, I've got to go; I've got something on the stove.'

'Please!'

'She's not here and I don't know when she'll be back. Next month? The month after? I've no idea.'

'Is she away, then?'

'Didn't I just say that?' the woman said crossly, glancing over her shoulder again.

'No, you just said she wasn't here. Do you know where she is?'

'No idea. I've only been working here a week.'

'Do you know if she's gone to Priory Hall?' Jamie asked.

'I'm not sure. I know she and her younger brother are staying with family in Essex. If you want to call back, Dr Kingsley'll be home later. I've got to find out the address anyway because a letter came for her and I'm supposed to be posting it to her.'

'A letter from Southampton?'

'Might be. What's it to you?'

'I sent it.'

She walked to the table and picked up a letter. 'This one?' She handed it to him.

The postmark said Southampton, although he didn't recognise the nurse's writing. But he knew it was his letter because he'd drawn two small snails in the bottom left-hand corner of the envelope.

'Yes, that's mine,' said Jamie. 'There's no need to post it. I'm going there now. I'll see Rae, if she's there, before the letter would arrive.'

'Well, you might as well take it then,' the woman said, closing the door.

It took longer that Jamie had expected to get across London to Fenchurch Street Station, and he was feeling tired by the time he boarded a train that would stop at Laindon. He found a seat and as he settled back waiting for the train to pull out of the station, he realised he was dozing off. It wouldn't hurt to sleep for a while, he told himself, so long as he didn't miss Laindon.

Two women got on the train and sat down near him, placing their baskets on the luggage rack.

'Honestly, Edna, I can't believe my Sadie and her kids've 'ad it so 'ard, what with the Blitz and everything,' the tall woman said.

'I know. They've 'ad more than their fair share of bad luck, that's for sure,' the woman called Edna replied.

'Still, at least Mr Hitler seems to 'ave given up bombing the living daylights out of them,' the tall woman said. 'Well, for the moment anyway. Who knows what's going to 'appen in the future?'

'I know, Vi. But at least we can 'elp out a bit. With all the food we grow. Your Sadie was so grateful for that veg,' said Edna.

'Yes. I know. Me and Alf moving down to Dunton were the best thing we've ever done, and we've got so much land to grow things. It's nice to be able to treat the family with fresh veg and fruit. Did I tell you that house we used to rent in Limehouse is a pile of bricks now? How's your daughter, by the way?'

'Fine thanks, Vi . . .'

The conversation continued, and other than the rather piercing laugh of the tall woman who was apparently called Vi, Jamie ignored them and dozed off again.

The shrill whistle roused him and he glanced around the carriage as the train chugged away from the platform. He was tired, and he considered standing up just in case he fell asleep and missed his stop, but Edna had jammed him in with one of her baskets.

'How's your Frank now?' Edna asked.

'Oh! He's distraught! That girl just up and left,' said Vi.

'Left? What! You mean she left Priory Hall?'

'Yes. Poor Frank! I told 'im there was no point holding a torch for her but it was too late. He was smitten.'

Jamie sat up at the mention of Priory Hall and listened in to the conversation. He was wide awake now.

'But I thought she told Frank she wasn't interested.'

'She did, but you know men. They don't listen, do they? He still thought he had a chance. I don't know what's wrong with the girl. He's a pleasant enough looking chap. And he's doing well for 'imself. But she didn't want to know.'

'Well, where did she go? Back to London? I hear that's where she was living before she moved in with the Richardsons.'

'No! You won't believe it — she's gone to New York!'

'No!'

'Yes! And what's more, she went to New York with some chap that turned up out of the blue!'

'No!'

'Yes!'

'Who was he?'

'I don't know. No one had ever seen him before. He just turned up and off they went, as bold as brass.'

'Are you sure?'

'Yes, I got it from Dorothy Moore. She went into Maison Marechal the other day and got it from that nice little French girl who works there. Apparently she and the girl used to spend a lot of time together.'

'Well I never!'

Jamie felt as though there was a weight on his chest and he was struggling to breathe. Rae had gone to New York! No, it couldn't be possible. But why not? She believed he was dead. She'd even attended the memorial service for him and the other men who'd died at Dunkirk. Why shouldn't she have met someone else? And why shouldn't she have gone to New York? She'd always wanted to travel.

'Are you all right, dear?' Vi said to Jamie. 'Only, it looks like you're finding it 'ard to breathe. And you've gone very white. Can I do anything?'

Jamie shook his head. 'No, no, thank you. I'm fine. But I couldn't help overhearing your conversation. The girl you were talking about, her name wasn't Rae, was it?'

'I don't know. I think it began with

an R . . . or was it an M . . . I'm not sure. Why?'

'I think I might have known her . . . once.'

'She didn't let you down too, did she? It looks like she's left a trail of broken hearts behind her. Good riddance, I say!'

Edna and Vi got their baskets down off the luggage rack when the train approached Laindon Station and as it stopped, they opened the door.

'You sure you're all right, dear?' Edna asked Jamie.

He nodded. He knew he wouldn't be able to speak.

'Are you getting out here, dear?' Edna asked him.

He shook his head.

There was no point getting out at Laindon. He'd carry on to Leigh and pay the excess on his ticket when he got there.

He felt like something inside him had died.

8

Rae looked out of her bedroom window at the lawns and gardens of Priory Hall. Beyond those lay the farmlands. It was a view that she'd often enjoyed with Miriam, who until just over a week ago had occupied the bedroom next door with her sister, Rebekah.

Rae missed the two German girls but especially Miriam, with whom she felt a special bond. She recognised the emptiness in Miriam and without confiding in each other, the two girls had somehow offered each other comfort. It wasn't until Rebekah managed to track down Karl, the boy with whom they'd escaped from Germany, that Rae realised why Miriam had seemed so empty and lost and who it was that she'd been yearning for.

The morning they left for New York, Rae had never seen Miriam so animated or so happy. Her face lit up whenever she looked at Karl, and Rae had felt the loss of Jamie even more than usual, despite being glad for her friend.

She'd decided to write a little every day about what was happening at Priory Hall, and as soon as Miriam found a place to stay and sent her an address, Rae would post her letter. Even better, Miriam had invited her to stay with them. It was going to be exciting to visit New York and of course to see Miriam, Karl and Rebekah again.

Rae got out the box in which she kept all Jamie's postcards and letters as well as the small carved boat, the snail shell and the handkerchief with the embroidered thistle. This disparate collection of things was all she had left to keep her memories alive. She didn't even have a photograph of Jamie.

One by one, she read the postcards and looked at the pictures. When the war was over, they'd have gone to New York together. And they would have kept going to Tokyo, Peking, Cairo,

Hong Kong — it wouldn't have mattered where; they would have made up their minds on a whim and have explored the world together.

One day, she would take off on her own. It wouldn't be the same without Jamie, of course. But there was nothing keeping her here and it wasn't like she'd miss home. She didn't feel she belonged anywhere, so she might as well simply keep moving.

But how much longer would the war carry on? A year? Two years? Ten?

Rae ran her finger over the embroidered thistle on the handkerchief, then held it against her cheek and closed her eyes, remembering.

All soft and fluffy, but underneath as prickly as . . . well, a thistle! Jamie had said to her when he'd given her the handkerchief after a holiday in Scotland.

It suddenly occurred to her that she'd never been to Scotland, and she longed to see all the places Jamie had visited when he was a boy.

As soon as she could, she'd visit Jamie's Uncle Gordon in hospital and find out where in Scotland the family had originated. She knew that Robert and Gordon MacKenzie had both come south together and had settled in Leigh-on-Sea, where they'd bought a boatyard, but when Robert met Jamie's mother and they married, the couple had moved away to the south coast where Jamie and his brother Alex had been born.

In fact, there were many places she'd never visited in England and Wales — places on her own doorstep. Perhaps now was the time to think about travelling. Not going on holiday, of course, but if she joined the Land Army, she might be stationed anywhere. And then when the war was over, she'd simply keep going.

And joining the Land Army would ensure her a wage. She knew from the girls who worked on Ben's farm they earned twenty-eight shillings a week, and although they had to pay for food and accommodation out of that, if she was careful, she could save a little.

There was also the *Wild Spirit*. Jack wasn't very keen on sailing and Joe was more interesting in flying, so Papa have given the boat to Rae. The *Lady Amelia* was still at Ramsgate where it'd been repaired and was awaiting someone to pick it up, but Papa had been too busy and Rae never wanted to see the boat again.

She wasn't sure she wanted to see the *Wild Spirit* again either, but at least the thought of it didn't bring back the chaos of the beach at Dunkirk and the image seared on her brain of Jamie standing shoulder-deep in water with his arm raised, sending her a kiss.

If she sold the *Wild Spirit*, it would raise money to help finance her travels. Although whether anyone would be interested in buying it while the war was raging, she had no idea. But first she would have to clean it thoroughly; then when she visited Jamie's uncle in hospital, she would ask him if he knew anyone who would be likely to buy. Perhaps he'd buy it from her and sell it for a better price after the war was over.

She added her new plans to Miriam's letter, folded it, and placed it back in her drawer ready to write more tomorrow.

Having made up her mind about selling the *Wild Spirit*, Rae decided to gather some cleaning things and cycle down to Leigh. Why not make a start on cleaning it up as soon as possible? She put the pail over the handlebars and filled it with brushes and cloths. Soap was rationed, so she didn't have any, but if she scrubbed hard enough she should make a good job of it.

She hadn't cycled through Hadleigh since the last time she'd met Jamie near the castle, and the sight of the ruins brought memories teaming back. The sooner she joined the Land Army and moved to another part of the country, the better it would be, she told herself.

* * *

Rae was having second thoughts about selling *Wild Spirit*.

Cycling through Hadleigh, seeing the stark remains of the castle where she and Jamie used to meet, walking through the narrow streets of Leigh where they'd once strolled and now looking at the dinghy which they'd sailed together, she felt overwhelmed.

There were too many memories and they were flooding into her mind, until it was brimming with images — and pain.

How many times had her eyes involuntarily settled on someone in a crowd who was the same height as Jamie or had the same hair colour or the same shape of face? And her heart had leaped. For a second, all the pain receded and she was awash with joy believing he'd returned. And then the realisation that it was someone else and that she would never again see Jamie slammed into her with renewed force. If only she could stop such wishful thinking, because it always left her feeling broken and empty.

She'd known the *Wild Spirit* would set her remembering, and it was because of that she was keen to sell it. Once it was gone, at least it wouldn't be a constant reminder. But when she reached the jetty and saw it rocking gently back and forth in the water, she began to wonder if she'd be strong enough to get rid of the one thing which had brought her and Jamie so much pleasure. She climbed aboard and leaning over the side, she dipped her hand into the water and closed her eyes, imagining.

There's no point clinging to the past, Rae, her inner voice told her. *If you're going to move into the future, you'll need to let go at some time.*

Rae sighed. It was true. If she wanted to travel, she would need money and the easiest way for her to do that was to sell the boat.

I will sell it, she thought. *But not yet.*

She didn't have the heart to start cleaning. What was the point? It would be a while before she was ready to part with the *Wild Spirit* and by that time, it would need to be done again.

She stared at the water swirling around her wrist, watching the ripples and wavelets, the shadows and highlights. It was mesmerising. Almost as if the water was alive. A living thing which had taken the one person in the world who she loved with her entire being.

Rae stood up and wiped her hand dry on her skirt. There was no point lingering in Leigh. If she was going to be miserable, she might as well go back to Priory Hall, to her bedroom or even better go to find the Land Girls and do something physical which would exhaust her and take her mind off her grief. She picked up the pail and clambered out of the boat.

Ahead of her, where the jetty met the road, three men stood talking. Rae wondered if any of them had known Jamie. Perhaps they'd even sailed to Dunkirk — and returned. She might even know them, but it was hard to tell.

The sun was shining in her eyes and the men were simply dark figures against the brightness.

They shook hands and two of them walked away, leaving the third at the end of the jetty.

Her eyes were playing tricks on her again, trying to convince her that the silhouetted man was Jamie. He was similar in height and he was holding his head to one side like Jamie used to, but this man was thinner, much thinner and his stance was different: he was leaning to one side. And when he stepped towards her, he limped. Rae looked away from him, not wanting to give in to wishful thinking and to believe it was Jamie, only to experience the agonising loss once again.

'Rae?'

She looked up in astonishment, because he even sounded like Jamie; and as the sun disappeared behind a cloud and she was no longer dazzled, and saw him clearly.

'Jamie!' The blood drained from her

face and she dropped the pail.

Rae ran to him and threw her arms around his neck. She had so many questions they tripped over themselves on her tongue. 'How? Where? When did you — ?'

'I thought you'd gone to New York,' he said, not attempting to answer her.

'Not yet,' she said, puzzled. His hands were on her arms; why wasn't he clinging to her like she was to him? 'How did you know I was going to New York?' she asked.

'So, you *are* going?' he asked, his eyes registering pain. 'I've found you just in time to say goodbye?' He placed his hands on her shoulders and gently pushed her away.

'Jamie! What are you saying? Why is this goodbye? You can't appear out of the blue and then tell me it's time to say goodbye!'

'But if you have someone else . . .'

'Someone else? Of course there's no one else! How could there be? There's only ever been you. There'll never be anyone else for me!'

'I think,' he said slowly, 'we might be talking at cross purposes. Somebody told me you had a sweetheart and you were going to New York with him.'

'Well, whoever it was, got their facts wrong!' Rae said crossly. 'Miriam and Karl have gone to New York and I'm going to visit them when they're settled.'

'So you haven't got a sweetheart?'

'That depends,' she said, 'on whether you'll have me or not.'

He frowned, then he said, 'I'm on my way to Uncle Gordon's. Will you come with me? You may want to change your mind about having me as a sweetheart.'

As they walked to his uncle's house, Jamie began to tell her what happened after the *Lady Amelia* had left him in the sea, and by the time he'd found the key under the mat and opened the door, he'd given her the main details. She'd listened intently to his story, but half of her mind was on his words: *You may want to change your mind about having me as a sweetheart.*

What was he going to tell her? He hadn't mentioned finding anyone else, but perhaps he was about to get to that part. Or perhaps after all he'd been through he simply didn't want her.

I can't bear it! she thought. *I won't bear it! If he doesn't want me, I'll go to New York on my own. I'll start again.*

'Rae, you're not going to punch me again, are you?' Jamie asked, and she realised her fists were balled and her teeth clenched. 'Only, I haven't got my strength back yet, and if you hit me, I might not be able to get up.' He hung his head. 'As you've no doubt seen, I walk with a limp. I'm not the same, Rae. Not the same as you remember. So if you want to, you can take it back about us being sweethearts. I'll understand.'

'Jamie, I never thought I'd see you again. I attended your memorial service, for goodness sake! Finding you alive is the most wonderful thing that's ever happened to me. Do you think a limp is going to put me off?'

'It's not just the limp, Rae . . . The wound has healed over now, but it's unsightly. In fact, it's repulsive.'

She kissed her fore and middle finger and placed them on his lips. 'Don't say any more. Nothing matters to me other than that you're here.'

'Rae, are you sure?' His eyes were now full of hope.

Putting her arms around his neck, she stood on tiptoe and kissed his lips, gently at first and then hungrily. She was shocked at how bony his shoulders felt beneath her hands. She would spend the rest of her life looking after him, and in time he'd regain his strength; but for now, he needed to know that she loved him and that she accepted everything about him.

Rae opened the top button of his shirt, but as she moved down to the next one, he caught her hand. 'Rae! What are you doing?'

'I think it's pretty obvious, Jamie MacKenzie,' she whispered, removing his hand from hers and undoing the next button. She kissed the skin she'd revealed, then opened the next button, placing a kiss further down.

'Are you sure this is what you want?' he asked, his breath coming in short gasps.

In answer, she slipped his shirt off and caressed his chest.

'I've never been surer of anything in my life,' she said. 'You will never, ever get away from me again.'

He unbuttoned her blouse and as he held her close, she shivered with pleasure as his naked body lay against hers.

'I want to feel every inch of your skin against every inch of mine,' she whispered, 'and I want to feel — '

Jamie placed two fingers against her lips to silence her. 'Then come with me,' he said, and led her to his bedroom.

Later, Rae awoke in bed, still wrapped in Jamie's arms, their legs entwined.

'Well, that was unexpected,' he said, stroking her cheek, 'but then you always were a wild spirit, Rae Kingsley! You've always taken me by surprise!'

'It looks like you've tamed me now!' She smiled and wriggled closer to him. 'You know, we fit together perfectly, just like the two shells of a cockle.'

He whistled a few bars of 'Molly Malone', and after they finished laughing, he held her tighter, 'I'll never let you go, Rae.'

She sighed with contentment. For so long, she'd yearned to find a place where she felt at home, and now at last, in Jamie's arms, she knew she belonged.

Other titles in the
Linford Romance Library:

HEARTS AND FLOWERS

Vivien Hampshire

Though her former partner is completely uninterested in his unborn child, heavily pregnant Jess can't wait to meet her new baby. However, she hadn't planned on going into early labour at the local garden centre! After baby Poppy arrives, the manager Ed visits the pair in hospital, and they strike up a friendship. Ed finds himself falling for Jess — but can't quite bring himself to tell her. Will the seeds of their chance encounter eventually blossom into love between them?

WHAT THE HEART WANTS

Suzanne Ross Jones

Alistair is looking for a very particular kind of wife: a country girl who would be happy to settle down to life on his farm in the small town of Shonasbrae. Bonnie, fresh from the city to open her first of many beauty salons, isn't looking for a husband and she certainly isn't accustomed to country life. With such conflicting goals, Alistair and Bonnie couldn't be less compatible. But romance doesn't always make sense, and incompatible as the two are, they don't seem to be able to stay apart . . .

THE JADE TURTLE

Margaret Mounsdon

When Jack and Alice split up, he broke not only her heart, but also their business partnership. Running their agency alone, Alice discovers that Lan Nguyen had, unbeknownst to her, contracted Jack to steal a jade turtle. Unable to refund Lan, Alice is expected to take on the job herself. Reluctant to commit theft, she finds an unexpected ally in Jack's brother Mike. Then somebody else steals the turtle first — and Alice and Mike must find out who!

HER FORGOTTEN LOVE

Elizabeth McGinty

When Elisa catches her partner in bed with another woman, she sets off for Italy to stay with her grandfather Stephano. Greeted at Verona airport by her childhood friend Cesare — now a handsome policeman — she learns that Stephano is ill in hospital, and just manages to see him before he passes away. Then she finds out that he has left her his beloved hotel. Can she make a new life for herself in Italy — perhaps with Cesare by her side?